Get Your
Coventry Romances
Home Subscription NOW

And Get These
4 Best-Selling Novels
FREE:

LACEY
by Claudette Williams

THE ROMANTIC WIDOW
by Mollie Chappell

HELENE
by Leonora Blythe

THE HEARTBREAK TRIANGLE
by Nora Hampton

A Home Subscription! It's the easiest and most convenient way to get every one of the exciting Coventry Romance Novels! . . .And you get 4 of them FREE!

You pay nothing extra for this convenience: there are no additional charges. . .you don't even pay for postage! Fill out and send us the handy coupon now, and we'll send you 4 exciting Coventry Romance novels absolutely FREE!

SEND NO MONEY, GET THESE
FOUR BOOKS FREE!

- -

C0582

MAIL THIS COUPON TODAY TO:
COVENTRY HOME SUBSCRIPTION SERVICE 6 COMMERCIAL STREET HICKSVILLE, NEW YORK 11801

YES, please start a Coventry Romance Home Subscription in my name, and send me FREE and without obligation to buy, my 4 Coventry Romances. If you do not hear from me after I have examined my 4 FREE books, please send me the 6 new Coventry Romances each month as soon as they come off the presses. I understand that I will be billed only $9.00 for all 6 books. There are no shipping and handling nor any other hidden charges. There is no minimum number of monthly purchases that I have to make. In fact, I can cancel my subscription at any time. The first 4 FREE books are mine to keep as a gift, even if I do not buy any additional books.

For added convenience, your monthly subscription may be charged automatically to your credit card.

☐ Master Charge   ☐ Visa
42101   **42101**

Credit Card #_____

Expiration Date_____

Name_____
(Please Print)
Address_____

City _____ State _____ Zip _____

Signature_____

☐ Bill Me Direct Each Month **40105**
Publisher reserves the right to substitute alternate FREE books. Sales tax collected where required by law. Offer valid for new members only. Allow 3-4 weeks for delivery. Prices subject to change without notice.

The
Danewood
Legacy

by

Jasmine Cresswell

FAWCETT COVENTRY • NEW YORK

THE DANEWOOD LEGACY

This book contains the complete text of the original hardcover edition.

Published by Fawcett Coventry Books, CBS Educational and Professional Publishing, a division of CBS Inc., by arrangement with Robert Hale Limited

Copyright © 1981 by Jasmine Cresswell

All Rights Reserved

ISBN: 0-449-50290-2

Printed in the United States of America

First Fawcett Coventry printing: May 1982

10   9   8   7   6   5   4   3   2   1

For My Mother,
With Love.

ONE

"Don't argue with your father. Please, Elizabeth, just this once, do whatever he orders you to do."

Elizabeth smiled at her mother but, with the skill of long practice, she avoided a direct answer. "Is my hair tidy?" was all she said.

"No," said Lady Barclay. "There is a curl by your left ear. If you come over here, I will scrape it back for you."

Elizabeth knelt by her mother's chair. There was no mirror in the schoolroom and she relied upon her mother to warn her if any curls had managed to work their way loose from the tightly-knotted twist of her hair. She felt Lady Barclay remove a steel pin from the heavy chignon and skewer the offending curls back into place.

"You didn't answer me, Elizabeth. It has been so peaceful this week. Could you not try to do what your father wishes?"

"I can certainly try." Elizabeth gave her mother a quick, affectionate hug. "Unfortunately, even my best efforts at obedience rarely seem to satisfy Papa."

Lady Barclay flushed. "He *is* your father, Elizabeth. It is your duty to strive to obey him in everything."

Elizabeth pulled a face. "It's so easy for you to say that, Mama, and so hard for me to do. Oh, Mama! Sometimes I am driven nearly wild by the boredom of living here!"

"It's because you're so clever," said Lady Barclay sadly. "It is a terrible burden for a woman to have such a lively intellect. It makes you so unsuited for the life a virtuous woman ought to lead."

Elizabeth gave a quick exclamation of denial, but they were interrupted by a knock at the door before she could speak. They heard the frightened voice of one of the parlourmaids.

"Miss Barclay, come quickly if you please! Your father is waiting."

There was no need for the maid to elaborate upon the need for haste. This was the second message she had carried up from the study, and they could both hear the note of panic in her voice.

Elizabeth ran to the door of the schoolroom, smoothing the folds of her black dress as she went. The harsh mourning of her outfit was unrelieved even by a touch of white, but on this occasion she was glad she wore no white collar or cuffs that might attract dust. She ran down the stairs and tapped lightly on the study door, feeling her heart beat with the mixture of fright and defiance that marked all her encounters with her father.

"Come in." The command was softly spoken. Sir

William Barclay had not achieved his tyrannous control over his household by raising his voice or losing his temper.

She pushed open the door, taking care to close it quietly behind her. She kept her eyes meekly downcast as she bent her knees in the childish curtsey her father still expected from his daughter.

"Did you wish to speak to me, Papa?" she asked.

He did not acknowledge her question directly, although the faintest of smiles touched his thin lips.

"I have sent for you because I wish to communicate the outcome of a recent conversation I have had with the Vicar."

Elizabeth searched her mind hurriedly for any possible misdemeanours she might have committed recently. There were several she could think of, but none she could imagine coming to Mr. Hodge's notice since she avoided the Vicar as much as possible. Besides, her father had spoken with a hint of satisfaction that was his equivalent of any other man's wild excitement. Sir William seemed to be waiting for some expression of interest on her part, so she said obediently;

"Yes, Papa?"

"You are nineteen years old, Elizabeth, and I have decided that it is time for you to prepare yourself for the establishment of your own household. I have always regretted the fact that your character is so unsuitably obstinate for a woman and I have always hesitated in the past to consider any arrangements for your future that would take you far from my supervision. However, Mr. Hodge has now suggested to me a most suitable opportunity for establishing you respectably in the world. He told me that he would be prepared to offer you the honour of sharing his life of Christian service to the people of this parish, and I have given him permission to come this evening and place his offer before you."

Elizabeth was too astonished to know immediately whether or not she was pleased at this chance to escape from her father's house. "An offer?" she asked. "Mr. Hodge wishes to employ me? Does he need another new governess for his children?" Mr. Hodge had four sly children, who always seemed in need of a governess. The prospect of teaching such children was not appealing, but Elizabeth suspected that nobody else could make life as bleak as her father, not even Mr. Hodge.

Her father's mouth thinned into a tight line of anger.

"I would not consider allowing a daughter of mine to serve as governess to another man's children. God has appointed us all to our appropriate stations and *your* station is certainly not that of a domestic in another household—however godly its head."

"Yes, Papa. I mean no, of course not, Papa." Elizabeth looked back down at the carpet.

Her father's voice fell harshly upon her ears.

"You are approaching maturity, Elizabeth, and should have realised that I spoke of your marriage. As a well brought up and virtuous woman, you know that it is your duty to provide comfort and solace to the man whom your family chooses as your husband. You have had many years to learn to admire and respect the noble qualities of Mr. Hodge's character. You will undoubtedly feel gratified that such a man has decided to honour you with a proposal that you should become his wife. When he calls upon us this evening, I trust that you will express your delight at the opportunity he is offering you."

"Mr. Hodge cannot want to marry me! He can't possibly think that we should suit!"

Sir William ignored the note of anguish in his daughter's voice, or else he didn't hear it.

"Maidenly modest is a becoming attribute in a young girl, Elizabeth. However, your station in life entitles you to expect a worthy man as your prospective husband."

"No!" The impulsive denial escaped before she could check it. "No, I won't marry him."

"I do not believe I have understood you, Elizabeth." She could hear the dangerous quiet of her father's voice, but the prospect of a lifetime tied to Mr. Hodge was sufficient to overcome all her other fears. "I won't marry Mr. Hodge," she said defiantly. "You cannot make me."

As soon as she had spoken, she recognized her mistake. Open defiance simply made her father more stubborn. Now it was too late to escape Sir William's anger and too late to escape the inevitable punishment. Her father's eyes had already hardened into glacial grey brilliance.

"Your opinion in this matter was not requested, Elizabeth, merely your obedience. You will receive Mr. Hodge this evening. You will accept the flattering offer he is planning to make to you. I anticipate that the marriage ceremony will take place in about two months."

He broke off to stare at her for a minute, his face lined with disapproval. He always found Elizabeth's flamboyant curls and sparkling eyes an affront to his sense of decorum.

"You will not join us for dinner this evening so that you may spend the dinner hour alone in the library," he said. "I trust you will pray for forgiveness for your unnatural and un-daughterly behaviour."

Tears sparkled on Elizabeth's lashes, but she held them back. Despairingly, she ventured one last appeal.

"Mr. Hodge is almost as old as you, Papa. He is old enough to be my father." She wondered if she should point out that marriage to Mr. Hodge would make her a step-mother to four children scarcely younger than herself.

Once again Sir William ignored the note of pleading in Elizabeth's voice. "Nothing in your behaviour has ever suggested to me that you are capable of disciplining yourself. Mr. Hodge is old enough, and wise enough, to provide you with the sober guidance that you need. I can only thank God that He, in His wisdom, has provided you with so suitable a husband. There is nothing further to discuss."

He turned his back, not even bothering to make sure that his daughter executed a suitable curtsey, usually one of his favourite topics for complaint. She nevertheless dipped into the obligatory bob before hurrying from Sir William's study.

She shut herself in the small family library. It was a cold, gloomy room, containing only those furnishings left behind by preceding generations of Barclays. No volume had been added to the shelves during Elizabeth's lifetime and, so absolute was Sir William's own lack of interest in the world of books, it had apparently never occurred to him that Elizabeth's frequent banishment to the library was actually one of her greatest sources of enjoyment. The Barclay ancestors, judging by their taste in literature, would not have found much in common with the present owner of Barclay Manor.

Elizabeth, when first locked in the library at the age of ten, had learned to wile away the hours of confinement by dipping into those books whose pictures or bright leather bindings held out most hope of entertainment. By the time she was twelve, she had abandoned such frivolous shelf-hopping and had started a methodical devouring of every title the library had to offer. She began on the lowest shelf in the far left-hand corner of the room and had by now progressed to the topmost shelf above the chimney-piece. Her opportunities for reading were only too frequent, since her periods of confinement increased with the passing of each year.

Since she was never able to discuss what she read, many of her studies raised more questions than answers, a fact which made her increasingly impatient with the narrow life at Barclay Manor. On balance, however, despite the occasional frustration, she had long ago decided that it was only the library that prevented her growing half-mad with boredom.

As she settled herself into the room's only comfortable chair and pulled a volume of Blake's poetry from the shelf, she wondered bleakly if Mr. Hodge had a library, or even a single novel in his vast, greystone vicarage. She started to feel hungry as the afternoon wore on, but she was well accustomed to missing dinner and had grown used to living with a temporary feeling of emptiness.

Fortunately, her hunger was usually short-lived. Her mother and the maids had long ago entered into a conspiracy to provide Elizabeth with food to replace the meals she was forced to miss. She did not know how the housekeeper accounted for the missing provisions and felt it better not to enquire. Lady Barclay was already torn between sympathy for her daughter's plight and guilt at disobeying her husband. Elizabeth had no wish to trouble her mother's conscience any further.

She often tried to convince Lady Barclay that she did not regard the long hours of solitary confinement as a punishment but her mother, who shrank from solitude, could not be convinced. She suffered when her daughter was shut in the cold library and, wrestling with her divided loyalties, she continued to bring her daughter food.

Elizabeth had frequently reflected that there seemed to be a certain lack of justice in a Divine system that caused the virtuous Lady Barclay to suffer pangs of remorse, while she escaped from her father's attempts at punishment with a full stomach and a stimulated intellect.

She closed the book of Blake's poetry with an angry thump. It was impossible to concentrate upon his writing, and equally impossible to turn her mind to useful thoughts of obedience. She had not known how fiercely she clung to the hope of freedom until today, when that hope had been swept away. She realised, now that marriage to Mr. Hodge loomed as a dreadful reality, that she had always nurtured the dream of escaping from her father through marriage. Some gallant suitor was supposed to materialize on the horizon and whisk her away to the delights of marriage and gaiety. London, and balls, and theatres and beautiful clothes had all appeared prominently in these secret daydreams. She pulled the hidden wishes from out of her mind, and tossed them scornfully away. What a foolish child she had been!

She did not notice the passage of time, nor did she hear the subdued sounds of the family preparing for dinner, so she was startled when a quiet knock at the library door was followed by the hushed voice of one of the maids. She stood up from the chair, easing the muscles she had allowed to become cramped during the hours of inactivity. She walked across to the door and rested her ear against its solid panels. Sir William did not allow raised voices, so this was a necessary strategy if she wished to hear what the maid had to say.

"Miss Barclay!" The maid's voice was even more subdued than usual. "Miss Barclay! Sir William will be coming in five minutes to unlock the library door. He says you are to go upstairs and change into your black silk dress. You may add a white lace collar and cuffs. He says you can look in your mirror, Miss, to do your hair."

"Thank you, Mary." Elizabeth saw nothing odd in receiving this lengthy list of instructions from the maid through a locked door. "You're quite sure about using the mirror?" she asked.

"Yes, Miss. You can take off the cover."

Elizabeth had a small mirror hung on the wall of her room. In order to discourage the sin of vanity this was covered by a velvet curtain. The rule of the house was that the curtain could be removed first thing in the morning in order to ensure a neat appearance during the day. All other preparations had to be made by touch alone, even dressing for dinner. Her father's permission for her to use the mirror, and to add touches of white lace to the mourning outfit she still wore in memory of her young brother, showed how much importance he placed upon Mr. Hodge's proposal. Elizabeth acknowledged silently that she might as well accept the idea of marrying Mr. Hodge. The marriage was as good as solemnized now that her father had made up his mind.

She heard the key turn in the library door a few minutes later, although Sir William did not deign to speak. She waited for his measured footsteps to fade into the distance and then walked quietly up the stairs to her room. She drew back the cover on her mirror, but she did not need to look into it to see that her face was deathly pale and her eyes were dull with resignation. She was nineteen, no longer a child, and she understood the realities of her life. She realised that it was one thing to defy her father in the secret escapades of childhood and quite another to oppose his wishes on such a serious matter as her marriage.

She scowled at her unhappy reflection in the tiny mirror. She wasn't sure whether she wanted to scream out loud or to laugh at the subtle ironies of fate. For years she had longed to leave Barclay Manor. But now her wish was about to be fulfilled in a manner that left her wondering if the cure was not likely to prove more painful than the original disease.

TWO

Her parents were already in the drawing-room when Elizabeth came downstairs, her black silk dress rustling over stiffly-starched linen petticoats. Sir William stood in a commanding position by the fireplace. Lady Barclay sat silently as always, her face shielded from her husband's line of sight by the high, upholstered wings of her chair.

Elizabeth waited submissively just inside the entrance to the drawing-room, although she knew that Sir William must be aware of her presence. Finally he spoke.

"Well, Elizabeth?"

"I am sorry, Papa, that my behaviour this afternoon gave you cause for anger. I will strive in future to think more carefully before I speak, so that I will not cause my mother needless pain."

Sir William accepted the apology with a ritual

nod of acknowledgment. He rarely listened to what other people really said, so Elizabeth doubted if he noticed the ambiguous phrases. Lady Barclay, however, was more acute than her husband and she glanced at Elizabeth with an expression of mingled warning and affection.

"You may ask your mother for some tea, Elizabeth," said Sir William. She felt her father watching her as she walked across the room to Lady Barclay's side. She accepted the small cup of tea with a smile of thanks as she saw her mother slip in a large lump of sugar and a generous dash of milk.

The tea was weak, but it was still piping hot and it felt refreshing after the long, cold hour in the library. She was relieved that her appearance had met with her father's approval, simply because it would make the evening more cheerful for the rest of the household. She hoped her unruly curls would stay put, so that her neat appearance would survive the proposal from Mr. Hodge unblemished by the frivolity of any forbidden ringlets.

Elizabeth sat down on the sofa and started work upon her embroidery. She was always pleased to sew quietly while her father read aloud to the family. Since she had by now heard the Holy Bible in its entirety at least ten times, she was able to listen with less than half her attention, while her thoughts roamed free and her fingers added exquisitely small stitches with surprising speed.

Occasionally Sir William varied his readings and dipped into a volume of collected sermons. Once he had started to read "Pilgrim's Progress", until he decided he could detect an unacceptable,

Non-Conformist tone to Mr. Bunyan's writings. Christian's progress was halted abruptly, just outside the Slough of Despond.

Tonight Sir William chose to read the familiar tale of Joseph and the pharaohs of Ancient Egypt. Elizabeth found the story of plague and famine all too brief. Far sooner than she would have wished, they heard the shuffling footsteps of their elderly butler, and Mr. Hodge was announced.

He came cheerfully into the centre of the room, rubbing his hands together to remove some of the chill of the March wind. It was a clear night, and the moon was high, but the walk through the night had left his nose red and his cheeks pinched with the cold.

He did not make the mistake of allowing the momentous nature of his call to divert him from any of the necessary civilities. He bowed long and low over Lady Barclay's hands, apparently overcome with joy at seeing her returned to health after her weeks of mourning. But his most profuse bows and his most unctuous compliments were reserved for Sir William. The living was, after all, in the gift of the Squire.

"My dear Sir William! How rewarding it is to observe such a splendid scene of family happiness and tranquillity! If only the other members of my parish could see the true contentment which rules this happy hearth, perhaps I might be able to persuade them to turn themselves from the false attractions of worldly vanity. Truly, I have only to step across the threshold of this house in order to know that I am in a home where every heart is lightened by the knowledge that Christian duty is here fulfilled to its utmost!"

Elizabeth had a long acquaintance with Mr. Hodge and his fulsome manner of speech. She normally beguiled the boredom of his visits by counting how many outright lies and how many smaller evasions of the truth she was able to detect in the course of his conversation.

This evening she was not in the mood for counting, and certainly not in the mood for laughing at the hypocrisy of his words. For the first time in her life, she was aware of feeling irritated by her mother. How could Lady Barclay sit comfortably in her chair, smiling serenely, her expression genuinely untroubled by the absurdity of Mr. Hodge's compliments? More important, how was she herself going to tolerate a lifetime of days and nights filled with such empty speechifying?

She turned her eyes back to her embroidery, sewing with fierce concentration, as if she somehow hoped that by making her stitches absolutely perfect she could create a talisman to deflect Mr. Hodge from his decision to propose.

It was useless, of course. He came over to her side and she felt his eyes resting on her face with such an expression as she had never before seen on any man. She did not recognize the hot impatience lurking in the depths of his pale blue eyes, nor did she understand why his eyes dropped suddenly to the black silk of her dress, stretched tightly across her bosom. She did not know why, but she knew that she squirmed, feeling an overpowering impulse to shield herself from his gaze.

Sir William cleared his throat, then stretched his lips into the nearest imitation of a smile that it was possible for him to achieve.

"I believe, Mr. Hodge, that you have called upon

us tonight for a special purpose. A purpose, I might say, which meets with my happy approval."

Mr. Hodge jumped to his feet from the sofa where he had been sitting beside Elizabeth. "Yes, yes! Yes, indeed."

His powers of flattery seemed temporarily to have deserted him and he sketched awkward, bobbing bows first in the direction of Sir William and then towards Elizabeth. Evidently fearing that Lady Barclay might feel herself neglected, he then bobbed a third bow in her direction adding another "Yes, indeed!" in case his general goodwill hadn't yet been made fully apparent.

Sir William, seeing that matters required his assistance in order to be brought to the desired conclusion, spoke testily.

"You may put your embroidery down, Elizabeth! Industry is all very well, but there are moments when we may all be allowed to put our efforts to one side. Come and stand by the fireplace!"

"Yes, Papa." She walked obediently to the stone hearth, wondering if it was permissible to receive proposals of marriage with one's eyes closed. Alternatively, perhaps she could simply stare over Mr. Hodge's shoulder—he was scarcely as tall as she was—and thus avoid any disconcerting glimpses of his wandering eyes.

Mr. Hodge regained his aplomb and seized her hands within his grasp. His fingers felt dry, the bones so brittle that she thought they might break if she squeezed them too strongly. She did nothing so unladylike, of course, but merely stood rigidly still, her hands limp within Mr. Hodge's grasp. She tried to fix her eyes beyond Mr. Hodge's face and at the same time avoid looking at her mother. She couldn't suppress a shudder as Mr. Hodge's dry wrinkled thumb caressed her wrist, and she knew her mother had seen her tremble. She forced herself to stand once more rigidly still.

"My dear Miss Barclay, your Papa, Sir William himself, has given me permission to speak to you upon a subject very dear to my heart. Over the years, Miss Barclay, I have watched your development closely. I think I may say that not even your father has expended more hours of loving concern in nurturing your youthful virtues. In my humble mission to the people of this parish I need a helpmeet, Miss Barclay, and I have asked myself who could be more suited as my lifelong companion than the woman whose character I myself have helped to mould? In short, Miss Barclay, I cast my hopes at your feet and ask that you will do me the honour of becoming my wife."

"I am honoured, Mr. Hodge, by your proposal." Elizabeth managed to proceed this far in her speech of acceptance before the words stuck in her throat. To her horror she felt the back of her larynx close tight in a fashion which made her gasp for breath. "I shall be happy..." She fought against the waves of nausea that threatened to overcome her. It was impossible for her to speak.

"We are waiting for your reply, Elizabeth." Sir William's bland words concealed a thread of steely determination that his daughter easily recognized. She tried once more to utter the necessary words.

"I shall be honoured to accept your flattering offer," she whispered.

"My dear Miss Barclay! Elizabeth, I may say,

with your permission?" He didn't wait for the anticipated nod of consent. "I beg leave, Sir William, to kiss my prospective bride."

Sir William looked less than pleased at this unexpected departure from the formality of the proposal, but he managed to give an austere nod of permission. "It is, I suppose, acceptable now that you are betrothed."

Elizabeth felt the pinched lips press against her cheek and she closed her eyes to shut out the revulsion that coursed through her. Her cheek felt wet from the imprint of Mr. Hodge's mouth, and she had to resist the impulse to reach for a handkerchief to scrub off the residue of his saliva. She wondered how often married people kissed. Surely it couldn't be more than once a day? To her horror she realised that Mr. Hodge was bending to kiss her other cheek and she pulled back, wrenching her hands away from him.

"No!" she panted. "No. I can't bear it. I *can't* marry you!"

To her astonishment, Mr. Hodge laughed contentedly. "How refreshing to find a young lady who retains all the innocent shrinking one must expect from a delicately-nurtured blossom such as yourself."

Sir William, whose experiences with Elizabeth had led him to a different interpretation of her refusal, spoke quickly to his daughter. "This evening's excitements have quite naturally overset your composure, Elizabeth. You have my permission to retire. You will wish to bid Mr. Hodge goodnight. I will make arrangements for him to join us with his children after Morning Service on Sunday. You will thus have the pleasure of sharing luncheon with your betrothed, and your future step-children. Goodnight, Elizabeth."

For once she hadn't the smallest desire to disobey her father's instructions. She could hardly wait to reach the sanctuary of her own room. She bade a formal goodnight to Mr. Hodge—the thought of calling him Clive was almost sufficient to bring a faint lightening of her mood—curtsied to her father and walked sedately across the room to kiss her mother. The formalities completed, she walked slowly up the stairs, her head meekly bowed, and as soon as the door of her room was shut she threw herself on the bed in a storm of weeping.

The memory of Mr. Hodge's dry fingers and lascivious kisses haunted her imagination. She wondered how she would ever resign herself to living in the same house as Mr. Hodge, knowing that there would be nowhere to hide from his attentions. Marriage to Mr. Hodge seemed unbearable, but it was impossible to imagine defying Sir William. Nobody had ever defied Sir William successfully, at least as far as she could remember.

She wondered briefly if she could enlist her mother's help, and rejected the idea at once. Lady Barclay would be willing to offer her daughter help, but her health and mental strength would never allow her to defy Sir William in such an important matter. In her whole life, Elizabeth had never felt so close to utter despair.

Somehow, somewhere between sobs, the idea grew in her mind that she would have to run away. If defiance was impossible, she could take refuge in escape. The thought of freedom stole into her heart, warming her with excitement until all the

24

practical difficulties began to occur to her. Where would she run to? What would she use for money? She had never in her life possessed more than a few shillings destined for the Church collection plate. Most of all, would she have the strength— or the selfishness—to leave her mother?

The difficulties of escape failed to deter her. She paced the floor of her room, racking her brains to think how she might best avoid discovery by her father. If she was going to run away, she had to be sure of succeeding in her flight, for she would never be allowed back inside Barclay Manor. She knew that her chances for escape were likely to be greater tonight than they ever would be again. Her father's vigilance was certain to increase as the day of the wedding came nearer.

With a sudden sharp toss of her head, Elizabeth stopped pacing the floor. The decision was made, the first mental steps taken. Now—tonight—it was time to go.

She didn't have to waste time wondering where she would run to. London, the fabulous city, marvel of visitors from all over the globe, beckoned her on. It was impossible for her to visualize London, other than as the exotic centre of all that was exciting and forbidden. The idea of seeking employment in such a vast metropolis ought to have been frightening, but she had no frame of reference in which to place her fears. The environment of Barclay Manor was so narrow that a weekend spent in the local market town of Reading would have seemed as much out of the ordinary as her decision to find work and live alone in the world's largest city.

Even the simple task of packing some clothes

presented her with problems. She had no valise or carpet-bag, not even an old-fashioned straw case in which to pack her possessions. No doubt there were boxes in the attics, but she would have no chance of fetching one unobserved. She stripped the pillowcases from her bed, pleased to see that the linen was new and strongly sewn. She folded as much clean underwear as would fit into one of the linen cases, and in the other she tucked a clean black bodice, a knitted black shawl, a hairbrush, a comb and her toothbrush. Since she had no idea what was and was not provided in lodging houses, it did not occur to her that her preparations were lacking in several essentials. She tied her two bundles into neat packages, and thought that she had overcome the problem of packing rather well.

Even her ignorance could not disguise the need for money. How much, she wondered, did it cost to live in respectable lodgings for a week? Would she be able to find work within so short a period of time? She knew that respectable and impoverished gentlewomen could become governesses, but she had no idea what other professions she could follow.

No amount of pacing up and down the room was going to produce any store of coins, and with a pang of regret she finally reached into a small casket on her bedside table. She pushed her grandmother's gold necklace and a handsome ivory broach into her reticule. There was no overcoming the fact that these, her only two pieces of jewellery, would have to be sold.

She waited for the hands of her small watch to pass midnight, then she threw on her heavy winter cloak, buttoning the fastenings at the neck with fingers that shook. She drew on her black doeskin gloves, normally reserved for Church on Sundays, and walked cautiously into the darkened corridor.

All the lights were extinguished and no sound wafted up the back stairs from the kitchen quarters. Elizabeth glided softly down the servants' staircase, her body pressed to the wall, her bundles clutched tightly in her arms. She felt that her shallow breaths were so noisy that they must surely wake the entire household and when one of the stairs creaked it seemed to her that the sound reverberated throughout the corridor.

She pressed herself more closely against the shadows of the wall. If she could just get out through the kitchen door, she could cut across the fields to the local train station. The few shillings she possessed would pay her fare to Reading, and in Reading she would sell her pieces of jewellery. She waited, dreading discovery, but the creaking stair passed unnoticed. The house remained as silent as ever.

It was such a relief to negotiate the stairs without being discovered that she crept into the kitchen already anticipating success. She was speechless with disappointment, therefore, when she closed the kitchen door softly behind her and looked up to find herself face to face with her mother. They stared at one another in silence.

It was Lady Barclay who spoke first. She put down her pen and pushed the ledger of housekeeping accounts to one side. "You are running away," she said flatly. "I guessed what you were planning to do, so I waited up for you."

Elizabeth's throat was tight with despair and

her reply emerged as a harsh whisper. "You mustn't stop me," she pleaded. "*Please* don't! I couldn't bear to marry Mr. Hodge."

Lady Barclay did not immediately reply. Her fingers toyed absently with the small pile of housekeeping coins on the kitchen table. "Where are you going?" she asked at last.

"I planned to go to London," said Elizabeth. "It seemed the most likely place in which to find suitable employment—and to escape discovery by Papa."

Lady Barclay closed her eyes, then pressed her hands to her temples as if to dull a throbbing headache. "There is so much that could go wrong," she murmured. "So many dangers lying in wait for somebody as innocent of the world as you. But it isn't fair to force you to marry Mr. Hodge."

She stared distractedly at the housekeeping accounts, although Elizabeth felt sure that her eyes saw nothing of what was on the pages in front of her.

With a sudden decisive gesture, Lady Barclay reached into the side pocket of her heavy black skirt and pulled out a small leather pouch. She scooped up the meagre piles of coins on the table and thrust them into the purse.

"Take this with you, so that you can pay for respectable lodgings. You will certainly need it." She seized one of the pens and scribbled a few hasty lines on a piece of paper. "Here," she said. "This is where my maid went to live when I married your father. She used to run a lodging house, and I know the neighbourhood there is respectable. Go quickly now, Elizabeth, before you are discovered." Almost to herself she added, "Whatever Sir William does, it will be worth it."

Elizabeth ran to her mother, more frightened by Lady Barclay's complicity in her escape than she would have been by threats of punishment.

"Why are you helping me?" she asked. "You never have before—not if it meant defying Papa."

Lady Barclay answered softly, but she could not conceal the anger that shook her thin frame. "I allowed your father to send my only son away to school, although we all knew that he was too weak to attend such a harsh boarding school. I was afraid to defy Sir William, and my cowardice killed my son. I cannot allow Sir William to destroy you as well. I no longer believe that it is always a woman's first duty to submit to her husband. I only wish that there was some more positive way in which I could assist you, but I have been cloistered in Barclay Manor too long. Goodbye, my dear, and take care." She went quickly from the kitchen almost as though she were afraid to continue the conversation with her daughter.

Elizabeth picked up the pouch, hardly able to believe her good fortune as she heard the chink of one coin against another and saw the red gleam of a golden sovereign. She pushed up the heavy iron bar that bolted the exterior door and walked out into the chilly night air. The wind dried her tears as they fell on to her cheeks and she scarcely knew whether she cried from sorrow at leaving her mother or from relief at escaping from Sir William and Mr. Hodge.

As soon as she was out of the kitchen garden her tears stopped and she drew a deep breath, revelling in the sensation of freedom. Commonsense quickly returned. She wouldn't be safe until she was hidden in London. She swung out confidently across the small orchard, walking towards the open fields of the Barclay estate. It was more than five miles to the nearest station, ten miles if she had travelled by road, and she needed to be waiting on the platform when the early-morning train drew in.

She tucked her skirts up around her waist and clambered over the stile, fighting against an impulse to burst into defiant song. London, she thought, and a smile wiped away the last trace of tears. London! I shall soon be there!

THREE

It was late morning when the train from Reading finally drew in to Paddington Station. The novelty of the journey, the speed at which the belching engine cut across fields, around villages and through narrow cuttings, had kept Elizabeth enthralled. She had travelled alone in a compartment reserved for ladies, and had managed to keep at bay all worrisome thoughts about what she would do once she arrived in London.

Stepping down on to the sooty platform, her bundles carried carefully under each arm, and her precious pouch of coins tucked into the pocket of her innermost petticoat, it was no longer possible to maintain her façade of confidence. She had never seen so many people gathered together in one noisy crowd. Her imagination, limited by life in a tiny village, had never even visualized so large a mass of heaving humanity. She stood on the centre of the platform, jostled by the crowds, buffeted by busy porters and small boys, but incapable of deciding which way to turn.

She did eventually walk in the general direction of the station exit, not so much because of conscious decision, but because the movement of the other people swept her inexorably towards the imposing gates of the station. She waited on the pavement, safely arrived at her magic destination, without the slightest idea of what she should do next.

A ragged boy, scarcely more than seven or eight years old, his clothes tattered to the point of indecency, came up and tugged at his cap. "Get you a hackney, Miss?" To her ears, accustomed to the soft burr of Berkshire speech, it seemed that he said "Getcher a nackney, Miss," and it was a second or so before she understood what he was suggesting.

She looked at him doubtfully. Her upbringing had impressed upon her that ladies never conversed with strangers, particularly strangers of the opposite sex. Moreover, the destitute, at least according to Mr. Hodge, were invariably rogues and vagabonds whose near-starving condition was caused by indolence and the refusal to perform honest work. The urchin's offer, therefore, should clearly be refused.

On the other hand, Elizabeth had no idea where to find a carriage to convey her to her destination. She mentally consigned Mr. Hodge and his strictures to the devil, and smiled at the urchin with such friendly radiance that his mercenary heart softened a fraction, and he decided to find her the cleanest hackney that he could.

Elizabeth held out two pennies. It did not occur to her that it would be more prudent to wait until the boy had actually procured a cab before offering him money.

"I should like a hackney," she said, still smiling at the lad. "Could you find a friendly driver who would take me to Drake Street? I believe it is near King's Place." She had taken the time to learn her mother's directions by heart.

The urchin struggled with his own years of professional training. Here was such an evident country bumpkin that it was almost against his personal code of honour to allow her to escape unfleeced. He scowled up into her sparkling blue eyes, and experienced a totally unfamiliar ache somewhere in the region of his stomach. "Bloody oysters was off," he told himself fiercely. "Shouldn't never have eaten them." He snatched the two pennies and ran round the corner to a line of waiting hackneys. He peered round furtively to make sure none of his cronies were observing this demeaningly honest transaction. He spotted Old Jake, waiting with his chestnut mare. Old Jake wasn't a bad fellow, and his horse was well-fed, although long past the age for pulling a heavy coach around town. The urchin sprang up on to the perch alongside the driver.

"Lady wants a hackney," he said briefly. "Proper flat, she is. Fresh up from the moors, I reckon. Take her where she asks, so that she's safe, or I dunno what's going to happen to her."

Old Jake obligingly whipped up the mare and trotted her around the corner. He spotted his customer almost immediately, and understood why the kid had gone soft on her. The style of her black clothes marked her as a lady, and the painfully unfashionable cut of her sombre outfit proclaimed its provincial origins. She stood out from the small groups of people around her not only because of her dowdy clothes, but also because of her stunning personal attractions. She had the most magnificent brown hair that Old Jake had ever seen. A huge, polished mass of it was gathered in a low knot at the nape of her neck, but a riot of curls had escaped from their pins and clustered around the edge of her heart-shaped face. Old Jake was shocked to discover himself lost in a daydream of what she would look like with all the hairpins removed, and the curls cascading over her naked shoulders.

He shook himself severely. He didn't have time for that sort of fancy imagining. Just at that moment, Elizabeth looked up and spotted the hackney. She smiled as she recognized "her" urchin squatting on the ramp. "Thank you," she said to him and then turned the same dazzling smile upon Old Jake. "Can you take me to this address?" she asked. She lowered her voice confidingly. "I am afraid that I don't know my way around London as yet."

"Get in," said Old Jake gruffly. He was a man of few words, little given to translating his emotions into explicit thoughts, but he did allow himself a brief shudder as he visualised what was likely to happen to this particular woman as she wandered about the city making such artless confessions.

But he could not spend time worrying about perfect strangers. It was beginning to drizzle with rain, and so far today he had hardly earned sufficient to pay for the horse's feed, let alone enough for his other expenses. He whipped up the mare with unaccustomed aggression, and headed the carriage swiftly across town.

Elizabeth, uncaring of the light rain, let down the carriage window and waved goodbye to the urchin, smiling her thanks. He scowled, shoved his hands into his pockets and proceeded to steal three muffins from Flash Fred's tray which, his professional pride restored, made him feel infinitely better. "She probably didn't have nuffink worth stealing," he reassured himself, and resolutely pushed aside all memory of that enchanting smile.

Old Jake prodded his weary mare through the crush of London traffic, halting the hackney in front of a row of well-kept houses. He swung down from his perch and went round to open the carriage door for his passenger. "Number twenty you want," he said. He added conversationally, "This is a nice enough district. Respectable like."

"Thank you." Elizabeth could see that the houses were well-kept and freshly painted, although they seemed narrow and gloomy to her country eyes. "How much do I owe you?"

"Half a crown," said Old Jake morosely. He had brought her safely to a respectable lodging house when he could have made a great deal more profit by taking her elsewhere. He felt it was not unreasonable to charge her double the flat rate for the journey.

She gave him the money with a smile, holding out some extra pennies. "Is that the right amount for a tip?" she asked. "I have never taken a cab before."

Old Jake accepted the money with a gloomy shake of the head. If this girl didn't get herself murdered before the week was out it would be a bloomin' miracle. "You don't want to go around London telling everybody you ain't never been here before," he said. "No telling who'll take advantage of a young thing like you."

"Well, you have not done so," said Elizabeth with what seemed to her to be irrefutable logic. "Besides anybody can see that I have never been in a big city before, so what's the use of pretending?"

Old Jake, recognizing the incontrovertible truth of this statement, gave a final shake of his head. "Got to be going, Miss," he said. "You go and give a good bash on the door of Number Twenty. I've been 'ere before, and the missis there will see you right." He sprang up on to his perch and hastened the horse out of the street. The sooner he got away from that particular customer, the better pleased he would be.

Elizabeth, amazed at the ease with which she seemed to be surmounting the hurdles in her path, walked slowly up the flight of stairs leading to the door of number twenty. The brass knocker was highly polished and the lace curtains at the window were white and crisply starched. She knocked briskly at the door, not bothering to squash her mood of self-congratulation. Surviving in London was proving a great deal easier than she had feared. She patted her petticoats, feeling the heavy pouch through the serviceable serge of her black skirt. She still had her money, her pillowcases were still neatly tied, and once she had washed her face and tidied her hair, she could set about the task of procuring some employment.

The door was opened by a plump maid in a huge canvas apron. "What do you want?" she asked aggressively.

Another caller might have been disconcerted by the lack of friendliness. Elizabeth, whose exposure to friendship and good-nature was strictly limited, simply accepted the maid's words at face value. She smiled cheerfully at the maid.

"I am looking for a room to rent," she said. "I have just arrived in London and I was particularly recommended to this lodging house."

The maid's features remained uncompromisingly grim, but her voice moderated its harshness. "I'm sorry, Miss. You're out of luck. All our rooms is taken."

"Oh." Elizabeth looked as disappointed as she felt. "Oh dear. I had not thought of such a possibility. My mother wanted me to come here because the owner used to be her maid. That was a long time ago, of course."

"This place has changed hands twice in the last ten years, Miss. Your mum obviously don't know much about London ways, expecting to find everything the same as it was twenty or thirty years ago. You're lucky the house is still standing."

Elizabeth looked so crestfallen that the maid's stern expression dissolved in a quick sigh. "Try around the corner in Ladbroke Grove," she said. "You can ask at number fifteen." She shut the door without bothering to hear Elizabeth's reaction to this piece of advice.

Elizabeth walked back down the stairs. Her feet, which had sped so willingly towards the front door only minutes previously, now dragged heavily from step to step. She had already walked five miles across the fields, and her toes suddenly felt cramped and aching within the confines of her black buttoned boots. Her stomach was also sending her fierce reminders that yesterday she had eaten no dinner, and this morning she had consumed only a cup of milk bought hastily on Reading station. Ladbroke Square—or had the servant said Ladbroke Gardens?—began to seem a long way away.

She plodded down the road, not sure which way she ought to be walking. Two or three carriages rolled by, but there was nobody walking in the street of whom she could ask directions. The prospect of plodding all the way to the end of this road, and then all the way back if Ladbroke Gardens turned out to be in the opposite direction, was not appealing. She was relieved, therefore, when she found herself in a pleasant square, more prosperous in appearance than the street she had just left. She saw the sign "Ladbroke Square" posted high on the side of one of the corner houses. This must be the place. She had been told to look out for number fifteen. She walked briskly along the pavement, her depleted energies reviving as she took note of the elegant Regency façade of the houses, and the attractive Queen Anne-styled windows. It was pleasant to think that her lodgings might be in such a pretty square, and she offered a silent message of thanks to her mother, whose purse made such lodgings financially possible. She even spared a moment of appreciation for her urchin, her cabdriver and the plump maid, who had all contributed to set her feet in the proper direction.

Number fifteen looked, if anything, even more elegant than the surrounding houses. Its front door was the same sober black as all the other houses in the square, but its porch positively gleamed with brass hangings, knockers, lamps, bell-pulls and even a brass urn containing a flourishing aspidistra preserved under glass. Elizabeth's spirits rose to their former level of optimism. She lifted the brass knocker, and beat a resounding tattoo on the door.

It was opened by a corpulent butler clothed in bright scarlet livery. His hair was powdered and curled in a style Elizabeth had never before seen outside the faded portraits in Barclay Manor. She stared uncertainly at this magnificent personage. Mama's purse could not contain sufficient money to buy many days' lodging in a rooming house that employed so resplendent a servant.

The butler had meanwhile completed his own rather startled inventory of the caller's appearance, and when she continued to stand silently on the doorstep, he spoke politely.

"Can I help you, Miss?"

"I have come about a room," said Elizabeth hesitantly. "I am looking for a job." She bit her lip nervously, annoyed with herself for revealing such personal information. Young ladies did not discuss their private lives with domestic servants, not even if they wore smart velvet liveries.

The butler subjected her to a second, and even more startled, scrutiny. "You've come *here* for a room, Miss? Who sent you?"

"It was the maid at number twenty," said Elizabeth, sufficiently flustered by the butler's manner to forget to add the name of the street. "She said that this house would probably have a vacancy for me."

"Have you worked before?" asked the butler, not bothering to mask his curiosity.

Elizabeth drew herself up with as much dignity as she could command, bearing in mind the two linen parcels under her arms, and the pinching toes of her new shoes. Social conventions in London might differ from those obtaining in the country, but surely butlers did not normally question lady visitors?

"I think it would be more appropriate if I discussed my plans with the proprietors of this establishment," she said haughtily. "I have no doubt I shall be able to provide suitable references if they are required."

The butler grinned. "That's one way of describing it, I suppose. You'd better step inside. I'll call Madam Portunio and see what she has to say. You can wait in the front parlour, while I fetch her."

Elizabeth followed the butler into the room he indicated. His manners, she decided, certainly did not match up to the splendour of his uniform. Indeed, he seemed deficient in most of the skills normally required by a butler. Even the parlourmaids at Barclay Manor would have known better than to conduct a conversation on the front doorstep. Perhaps she could afford to stay here after all. Such an ill-trained butler could not command very high wages, and the rooms might be quite reasonably priced.

This matter settled, she sat down gingerly on the edge of the chair the butler indicated and surveyed the parlour. The landlady evidently had a passion for scarlet. Heavy red velvet curtains draped the windows and were looped back with gold silk tassels. The tables were covered in long red chenille cloths and even the chairs were upholstered in a bright scarlet material that almost matched the butler's livery.

Accustomed to the sober brown leather of Barclay Manor, and the faded homespun and horsehair of the Vicarage drawing room, Elizabeth found the red parlour amazingly cheerful. She had never seen the inside of a theatre, but she had always imagined that a playhouse would have just this sort of opulent and glittering magnificence. A spur of excitement quickened her heartbeat. It would be fun to stay in this house, just for a little while, and explore the historic attractions of the capital city.

Her reflections were interrupted by the arrival of the landlady. Madam Portunio, soberly clad in a purple crinoline of modest size, entered the parlour briskly, but she stopped short at the sight of Elizabeth.

"What is this, Peterson?" she asked the butler. "I do not have time for the funny jokes."

The butler replied stolidly. "She says she wants to work here. She said Maisie, down at number twenty, sent her over." .

"It is true?" Madam Portunio turned her flashing black eyes in Elizabeth's direction. "You are looking for work in my House?"

"Not necessarily *here*," said Elizabeth, wondering if all Londoners were as strange as these two. "Indeed, I did not know that you had any actual employment opportunities here. I was merely looking for a room."

"If you take a room here, you work for me. What do you think this place is? We are the finest House in London, and don't you forget it, my girl. Kate Hamilton herself don't have any smarter girls than me!"

"I am sorry if I have offended you," said Elizabeth. "I have always lived in the country up until now, and so I don't know much about London ways. I was hoping somebody would be able to teach me." She had never looked for a room in a lodging house before, of course, but nevertheless she could not help feeling that the course of this conversation was a little strange. She got up from the chair, and once again tried to gather the tattered shreds of her dignity.

"Perhaps you would be good enough to show me the room you have available, and then we might be able to discuss terms."

A small gap in the red velvet curtains permitted a single ray of sun to enter the cozy parlour, and as she stood up, Elizabeth's face and figure were illuminated in the beam of sunlight. Madam Portunio smothered a soft gasp, turning it quickly into a convincing cough.

"Why do you wear those clothes?" she asked abruptly. "If you were properly dressed, you could name your own price. And I do not make such remarks to many of my girls, that you may believe!"

"Name my own price?" repeated Elizabeth in bewilderment. "Name my own price for what?" She looked at Madam Portunio and the butler, the conviction growing upon her that she had wandered in to the home of two lunatics.

Madam Portunio turned angrily to the butler. "I told you there had been some mistake, Peterson! You, young woman, whatever your name is, what do you think this establishment is, for heaven's sake!"

"I was given to understand it was a rooming house," said Elizabeth stiffly. "I am looking for respectable lodgings, but I am sorry to have troubled you if there has been some misunderstanding."

The butler did not manage to conceal his snort of laughter, but Madam Portunio stared at Elizabeth with intense calculation. "This is not a lodging house," she said. "But I think, nevertheless, that I might be able to provide you with just the job you are looking for. You *did* say you were looking for work?"

Elizabeth nodded, but she did not sit down again. However tired her feet might feel, she was anxious to escape from these peculiar people.

"Peterson!" Madam Portunio spoke with sudden decisiveness. "Fetch us a bottle of... That is to say, make us some tea, and perhaps a few slices of bread and butter. We have things to discuss Miss... What is your name, my dear?"

"Miss Barclay," said Elizabeth, then wondered if it might not have been wiser to invent a different name.

"Pray be seated, my dear Miss Barclay. There has been a little misunderstanding between us, no? But Peterson shall bring us some refreshments, and I will explain to you my very good idea for your future employment. Then I will show you a room I have available." Madam Portunio smiled kindly. "I shall be happy to allow you this room, free of charge, in return for your services to my establishment."

Elizabeth sat down. Lunatics or not, the prospect of tea and bread-and-butter was definitely enticing, all the more so if she needed to leave and start searching the streets for another lodging house. She perched warily on the edge of one of the overstuffed chairs. "If this is not a lodging house, Madam, then what is it? And what sort of work do you have in mind?" She did her best to look lofty and high-minded, something that her clusters of curls always made very difficult. "I was planning to seek employment as a governess," she said.

Madam Portunio did not bother to comment on the improbability of any mother hiring a governess who looked like a cross between the goddess Venus and Helen of Troy. "You will find my work more enjoyable," she said with conviction. "Ah, Peterson! Bring the tray to Miss Barclay, please." Madam Portunio smiled confidingly to Elizabeth. "My hands have become a little stiff," she said with sublime disregard for the truth. "I should appreciate it if you would be so good as to pour out our tea."

Elizabeth willingly complied, and Madam Portunio noted with great satisfaction the fragile bones of Miss Barclay's wrist, the long, tapering fingers and the ladylike confidence with which she performed the social ritual of pouring tea. Her plan, conceived in a flash of genius, was certainly going to be a success.

Elizabeth nibbled at a thin slice of fresh bread,

and yearned to help herself to another piece. Determined to avoid such a breach of good manners, she waited hopefully for Madam Portunio to suggest a second helping. Her hostess was preoccupied, however, and soon broke into a beaming smile.

"You will wish to know what work I have in mind for you, Miss Barclay." Madam Portunio's sharp black eyes scrutinized Elizabeth's face. "I am the owner here of a club. It is most exclusive, and the gentlemen come here to relax over a glass of wine and a game of cards before returning home to their families."

"Oh," said Elizabeth, unable to think of any more intelligent remark. She had read a little about the London clubs for gentlemen and knew that her father did not approve of them. Her great-grandfather had been a member of Waitier's and Sir William had once suggested that a great deal of the Barclay family fortune had been gambled away at Waitier's tables. She looked cautiously round the empty parlour and listened to the quietness of the house.

"There do not seem to be many members present just at the moment," she ventured to say.

Madam Portunio smiled reassuringly. It seemed to Elizabeth that Madam Portunio smiled rather a lot. "My clients...that is to say, the members of this club prefer to come here later on in the evening. During the day they must attend to the needs of their families and to the affairs of their estates, no? Even in the country, I am sure you realise that the gentlemen are kept busy during the day."

"I suppose so." Elizabeth could hardly confess

that her experience of what gentlemen did was limited to two examples. "I wish for employment because there is nobody else to support me, but I do not think I could be of much use in your club, Madam Portunio. I am afraid that I have never played cards and would not know how to conduct myself in a gaming establishment."

Madam Portunio did her best to mask her gratification at learning Miss Barclay was alone in the world. She certainly didn't want irate parents descending upon her, demanding restitution. "That is of no consequence, my dear Miss Barclay." Madam Portunio swept away Elizabeth's ignorance with a wave of her hand. "I do not wish you to play cards. I wish you merely to greet my guests as they arrive and to be on hand to serve them tea and other refreshments if they should require it. Little tasks of that nature, you understand."

"That does not seem a very demanding occupation," said Elizabeth doubtfully. "Why do you think I am especially suited for the work?"

For once Madam Portunio was able to reply honestly. "You are very beautiful," she said. "Naturally I prefer that my members should have something pretty to look at. That is only fair after they have expended their energies during the day, struggling to care for their families, do you not agree?"

Elizabeth's personal experience did not suggest that gentlemen expended their energies during the day in a ceaseless struggle to provide for their families, but she smiled politely, her mind busy planning. Perhaps she could accept a job with Madam Portunio while she looked for other, more suitable employment?

"Come!" said Madam Portunio with sudden determination. "I shall show you your room, and you may decide whether or not you wish to accept my offer." She swept regally from the parlour and conducted Elizabeth past a marble staircase, edged with gilt-painted bannisters. Elizabeth thought she had never seen anything half so splendid in her entire life. Madam Portunio paused at a second flight of stairs, considerably more modest than the first, but polished and carpeted so that Elizabeth knew there must be a third flight of stairs for the servants.

"This is a very large house," Elizabeth said, unable to disguise a note of awe in her voice.

"Yes," said Madam Portunio, ushering her hurriedly up the stairs. "And here is the room which would be yours."

Elizabeth could not keep back the unladylike gasp of amazement. The room was quite small but the floor was covered with thick, rich carpets, and the huge bed was draped in a padded spread of shiny pink satin. It was not the furniture, however, that had caused Elizabeth to gasp. It was the fact that two walls of the room were covered in mirrors, so that the room and its occupants were reflected back and forth in a seemingly endless series of reproductions. Elizabeth stared at her shimmering reflections. It was the first time she had ever seen herself full-length, and she was amazed by the sight of her own black-draped person. Quite forgetting Madam Portunio, she went up close to the mirror and peered at herself in silent astonishment. She had had no idea that her body curved in quite such an extraordinary fashion. She blushed at the thought. Ladies did not think about the curves of their bodies, much less stare at themselves in double mirrors.

"It is a very...pleasant...room," she said uncertainly, wondering how she would ever manage to fall asleep under so many layers of satin hangings.

"And it shall be yours," said Madam Portunio quickly. "Remember, it is free of charge and I will pay you two pounds a month in addition."

"Twenty-four pounds a year?" Elizabeth knew that this was more than any governess could hope to earn, and she was startled by Madam Portunio's munificence.

"Wages are higher in London," said Madam Portunio quickly, and smiled yet again. "I take it that we are agreed? And you will start work tonight, no?"

"Yes," said Elizabeth and wondered why she felt so frightened. "But are there no other employees who could help to explain my duties?"

"You will meet some of my girls this evening," said Madam Portunio. "That is to say, I have a large family, and many of my relatives send their daughters and nieces to help with my little establishment. Some of them still speak English with a strange accent, because I am come from Italy, no?"

"I see," said Elizabeth. She had wondered if Madam Portunio was a foreigner, or whether her alien manner of speaking was simply a further example of the peculiarities of London. Perhaps, since Madam Portunio was a foreigner, it explained some of the strangeness of her ways.

"There is just one more thing," said Madam

Portunio, pausing in the doorway. "I shall send up one of the maids with some water so that you may take a bath. She will also provide you with a dress to wear this evening." She held up her hand as Elizabeth started to protest. "No, my dear Miss Barclay, say nothing. You will do me a favour if you agree to wear it. I bought it for my dear little niece and I am afraid she never lived to wear it." Madam Portunio whisked a hand across her eyes and her voice choked on a little sob. "The fogs of the London winter you will understand. So hard for a child of the sunshine. Poor little Teresa!"

"Well, if you wish me to wear it, Madam Portunio." Elizabeth could not help feeling rather excited. For the last nine months she had been wearing mourning clothes for her brother, cut out from pieces of material bought many years previously by her grandmother. She decided that she was doing so many things that would shock and horrify her family that accepting a new dress from her employer seemed hardly significant.

"The maid will bring you the new dress and something to eat. You had better come downstairs about nine o'clock. That will give you time to introduce yourself to my other girls." Madam Portunio gave yet another of her swift smiles. "That is to say, my relatives and some of their young friends." With a last sharp glance from her piercing black eyes, Madam Portunio swept out of the room.

Elizabeth sank into the armchair by the fireplace. New clothes, huge mirrors, pink satin bedspreads and twenty-four pounds a year of her own. No wonder her father complained that all his agricultural labourers kept leaving for London! She stretched out in the chair, worn out by all the excitements of the day. Within two minutes, she was fast asleep.

FOUR

Madam Portunio had expected a transformation in Miss Barclay's appearance. In her efforts to recruit only the very best girls for her establishment, she had long ago learned to pick out the rare piece of gold from the unpromising lumps of clay that were constantly offered for her selection. Even so, she could scarcely conceal her gratification when she saw her newest recruit floating delicately down the gilded staircase.

Miss Barclay wore a dress of pure white organdie, modestly cut and decorated with white silk roses around the hem. Her neck, free of any jewellery, was graced by clusters of dark ringlets that fell from the soft twirls of her chignon. Her blue eyes shone out beneath delicately arched brows and her unpainted complexion was without blemish.

Madam Portunio, who believed in being well

prepared, had bought the dress ready for the next time she had a convincing virgin on hand, but she had never really expected to achieve such a marvellous combination of innocence, stunning beauty and—best of all—obvious gentility. For a few moments, as Miss Barclay descended the stairs, she allowed herself to indulge in delectable financial day-dreams. Once Elizabeth had been seen by all the wealthiest clients, Madam Portunio would conduct a discreet auction. She had no doubt at all that every one of her customers would be competing for the privilege of taking the virginal Miss Barclay to bed. Entrancing figures danced through Madam Portunio's head. Perhaps a thousand pounds would not be impossible?

The prospect was so agreeable that Madam Portunio greeted Elizabeth with a smile of unmistakable and radiant friendship.

"My dear, you are looking charming! You will be a graceful addition to my little club."

"Thank you," said Elizabeth doubtfully. She felt indecently exposed in her new gown. The neckline, which Madam Portunio considered so modest, struck Elizabeth as verging upon the scandalous. However, she did not quite know how to tell her employer that she felt under-dressed, so she shuffled a little awkwardly in her new satin slippers. "Wh-what *exactly* am I expected to do?" she asked.

"Come." Madam Portunio led her swiftly into the familiar red parlour. "I would like you to meet some of my other girls...That is to say my dear little cousins and nieces." She swept into the middle of the parlour and said severely, "Girls! Here is our new companion, the one I told you about.

Daphne, you are to take Miss Barclay under your wing."

A generously-curved young woman, with enchantingly-dimpled cheeks, disengaged herself from the group and came over to Elizabeth's side.

"Well, Miss Barclay love, are you ready to tackle the lions? I expect there are some hungry ones waiting in the supper room."

The girls tittered and Madam Portunio flashed a glance of furious warning at Daphne. "You will remember what I told you about Miss Barclay, my dear *cousin*, and help her to serve our kind members just as she would her own dear father."

"Don't worry," said Daphne, "We shall conduct ourselves like nuns at a Church supper."

Elizabeth paid no attention to Daphne's remarks. The mere mention of the word "father" had been quite sufficient to overset all her powers of concentration. Conscious of a small silence, she tried to drag her eyes away from the splendours of Daphne's gown. The royal blue satin crinoline was draped in swathes of blond lace and the neckline plunged in a fashion which caused Elizabeth to stare in hypnotized fascination, blushing as she did so. Perhaps Miss Daphne did not realize exactly how much of her anatomy was visible to anybody taller than herself?

Now that the moment of starting work had arrived, Elizabeth was assailed by doubt, but Madam Portunio patted her arm reassuringly, still smiling with every appearance of friendship. Her girls viewed the smile with varying degrees of cynical amusement. The Old Devil clearly expected a fat profit from this unsuspecting pigeon.

"Just remember, Miss Barclay, that you should

stay close to my cousin Daphne's side. She will see that you do all that you should, and nothing that you should not. Nothing could be easier, you will see." Madam Portunio's sharp little eyes flashed towards Daphne. "Watch the booze, girl! That is to say, make sure that our gentlemen don't encourage Miss Barclay to drink anything stronger than tea!"

Daphne's brown eyes were tinged with contempt. "Don't worry, *Cousin*. Your investment will be safe with me." She led Elizabeth out of the parlour.

"You speak most excellent English," said Elizabeth, anxious to be friendly towards her supervisor. "Have you lived in England for a long time?"

"Oh...er...a couple of years, you know," replied Daphne, who had never before had her Cockney tones mistaken for a foreign accent. "This is the supper-room," she announced with some relief. "Get ready to smile because I expect it's full of the old b...our gentlemen friends."

She pushed open the door to a spacious room containing several white-clothed tables and a sideboard groaning under an imposing array of silver tureens. Groups of gentlemen sat around the tables and to Elizabeth's bewildered eyes it appeared that her services could hardly be necessary. There were already four or five girls hovering around the tables, offering to fill glasses or occasionally handing round plates of food.

Dahphe's arrival was greeted with a general shout of pleasure. At least three of the men jumped up from their seats and placed smacking kisses on her cheek. The men who did not kiss her remained lounging in their chairs, a fact Elizabeth found almost more shocking than the casual kisses of greeting. The men looked like gentlemen, so surely they knew they had to stand up when ladies came into the room?

A pleasant-looking young man with sandy hair and a monocle that grotesquely enlarged the size of his left eye, glanced up from his wineglass and stared at Elizabeth. He smiled at her with such open admiration that she could not help smiling back. He sprang to his feet and came over to her side.

"You're new here," he remarked amiably. "Where did you come from? I am Jack, and if I'd known you'd joined Madam Portunio's selection of lovelies, I'd have come calling sooner!"

"How do you do, Mr. Jack?" Elizabeth acknowledged the introduction. "I am Miss Barclay and I just arrived today."

A burst of laughter roared out from Jack's table companions as he found himself shaking Miss Barclay's demurely-gloved hand. Daphne called out cheerfully, "Watch what you say, Jack! Miss Barclay isn't available for the usual services so you'd better keep a guard on your tongue. She'll bring you tea and supper, but anything else you might be wanting you'd better look elsewhere. You can't afford what the Old Devil will be asking for her."

Jack looked crestfallen, but sighed resignedly. "The sooner Uncle Charlie kicks the bucket and leaves me some of his ill-gotten gains, the better pleased I shall be. At least come and sit with us, Miss Barclay, and tell me what you're doing here."

Elizabeth sat down. Her head reeled from the constant assaults upon her understanding. Did nobody in London behave in the fashion she had learned to expect in Berkshire? She had known that her own circle was particularly narrow, but was all the rest of the world like this strange establishment run by Madam Portunio? Perhaps, after all, her father was right in asserting that London was the sink of vice and the natural enemy of all virtue. She had been taught to equate virtue with solemnity, so that she could only conclude all these people were far sunk into depravity. They were far too cheerful to be burdened by guilty consciences.

An elderly man, enormously fat, stopped his consumption of veal and ham pie long enough to glance at Elizabeth with a cheerful wink and she smiled back before realising they had not been introduced. He reached for a napkin and gave an exaggerated sigh. "Well, I've got Madam's price for you, but I doubt if I'd have the energy to take advantage of my purchase." He grinned ruefully as Daphne brought him a huge helping of sliced pheasant. "Ah, girl, you'll have me asleep before I get any one of you upstairs. I swear Old Portunio provides the best suppers in London!"

Elizabeth smiled at him politely, although she didn't understand what he was talking about. The conversation around the table became general and she courteously answered the many questions that were put to her, taking care to conceal the location of her family home and the identity of her parents. She had no idea why many of her answers seemed to provoke such merriment around the table, but she was relieved to find that she could keep Madam Portunio's guests entertained with so little expenditure of effort.

The occupants of the supper-room changed with

a certain regularity. Some of the gentlemen disappeared and so did some of the girls. The girls seemed to return, however, whereas the gentlemen did not. Daphne remained close to Elizabeth and, although Elizabeth was starting to feel tired, she could not say that she was finding her work unpleasant.

Madam Portunio came into the supper-room when Elizabeth had been entertaining the guests for almost three hours. She seemed pleased with the progress of events and patted Elizabeth approvingly upon the arm. "You are doing well, Miss Barclay. I am pleased with you." Her words of praise were interrupted by one of the servants, who spoke softly to Madam Portunio.

"There is a man who wishes to have a word with you in private, Madame."

"Who is it?" Madam Portunio was too busy to waste precious moments on any but her most important clients.

The servant coughed discreetly. "It is Lord Danewood, Madame. I do not think he is prepared to wait long."

"Lord Danewood!" exclaimed Madam Portunio. "Miss Barclay, find the butler and instruct him to bring some refreshments to my private parlour." She swept out of the room before Elizabeth could acknowledge the order.

Elizabeth was quite relieved to escape from the boisterous atmosphere of the supper-room, even if it would only be for a few moments. There was no difficulty in finding the butler, since he was stationed prominently in the hallway, an even more impressive figure this evening than he had been earlier in the day. His scarlet livery was adorned with a sumptuous array of gold braid and golden tassels. Elizabeth thought that no other butler could ever have been so magnificently clad. She approached him diffidently.

"Madam Portunio would like you to take some refreshments into her private parlour."

The butler gave a sly grin. "I thought she'd be chuffed when she found out Lord Danewood was here. Never set foot in the place before. But he's had the accident now, of course." He saw Elizabeth's puzzled expression and cut off his flow of confidence abruptly. "I'll take in a tray of refreshments now, Miss."

She sank down on to a hall chair and closed her eyes for a minute, grateful for the relative quiet of the hallway. She was so deep in her own confused thoughts that she jumped visibly when Peterson returned from the parlour and spoke to her.

"Miss! Miss Barclay! Old Portunio wants to speak to you in her parlour." He smiled at some secret joke. "She seems to think Lord Danewood might have a job for you, although if you ask me, it'd be a waste of your smashing looks." He cut himself off again. "Quickly now, Miss. Straighten your sash."

Elizabeth knocked on Madam Portunio's door, waiting nervously for permission to enter. When she walked in, she saw her employer standing by the fire, her face all beams and smiles although Elizabeth was aware of some unspoken tension that stretched around the room.

"Miss Barclay! Come in, come in!" Madam Portunio's voice sounded less confident than her words and Elizabeth advanced hesitantly towards the centre of the parlour.

"Perhaps, my lord, you would care for some port? And I believe that there is also some excellent brandy on the tray," said Madam Portunio.

"Some brandy would be pleasant." Elizabeth's head jerked up in dismay at the sound of Lord Danewood's voice. It was icy cold, despite the superficial courtesy of his words. The chilliness reminded her of her father, and she shivered involuntarily, looking at the visitor through lowered lashes. He was a tall man with dark hair, but his chair was placed in the shadows cast by the old-fashioned chimney piece and she found it hard to form any clear impression of his face and figure.

"Please pour Lord Danewood some brandy, Miss Barclay." Madam Portunio's sharp request brought her back to a realization of her duties. She did as she was told and walked over to Lord Danewood's chair, holding out the glass of brandy. When he made no move to take the glass, she said quietly, "Do you wish to have this brandy, my lord?"

She felt him stiffen slightly at the sound of her voice, but he merely gestured curtly. "Put the glass on the table by my side."

Once again Elizabeth did as she was bid and moved back to the middle of the room. Innately courteous, she spoke politely to her employer. "Would you care for something, Madam Portunio? There are some macaroons on the tray if you would care for them."

"No, no. Nothing. I have already eaten this evening." Madam Portunio turned to Lord Danewood, her manner a curious compound of doubt and triumph.

"Well, my lord! You have heard her speak now and you can begin to guess what a treasure she

59

is. Put any questions that you wish to her. You will find that I have not been exaggerating her value."

Lord Danewood did not even glance at Elizabeth. He spoke indifferently, as though she were not present. "What does she look like?" he asked.

"Beautiful," said Madam Portunio dryly. "And every inch a lady which is what you require."

"I should appreciate a few more details. You will realise that the word beautiful can—and usually does—cover a multitude of different traits."

"Dark hair, naturally curly. Violet eyes. A complexion of stunning purity. Tiny waist. Slender fingers."

Lord Danewood did not seem to find the description sufficiently interesting to make the effort of turning his head.

"What is your name, young woman?" he asked.

She was almost angry enough not to reply. "Elizabeth Alice Barclay," she said at last, seething with fury at Madam Portunio's insulting catalogue of her attractions. She could not quite contain her resentment. "I cannot think, my lord, that it is the act of a gentleman to discuss a lady's personal appearance as though she were a horse whose finer points must be analysed."

"That is possibly true, Miss Barclay. Although much may be excused to a gentleman who is blind, do you not think?"

Elizabeth gave a small gasp. "I beg your pardon…I had not realized, my lord…It was not possible to discern…"

"You are perhaps struggling to say that you had not observed my deformity, Miss Barclay?"

"I do not consider blindness a deformity, my

lord," said Elizabeth stiffly. "An affliction, certainly, but not one which excuses its victims from all the normal courtesies."

Lord Danewood gave a sudden laugh and when he spoke again his voice was slightly warmer. "Your current situation has not yet taught you the neccessity of humility, Miss Barclay."

"Why should it, my lord? I am independent here, earning my own living. I consider the situation a matter for pride rather than humility."

"An original view," said Lord Danewood dryly. "Come and kneel in front of me. I wish to touch your face."

Elizabeth walked reluctantly across the room and knelt in front of Lord Danewood's chair. Now that she was so close to him she could see that he was younger than she had imagined, no more than thirty-five. His eyes were concealed behind dark-lensed spectacles that successfully masked his eyes. She trembled when she felt his hands reach out to touch her forehead and then trace the delicate outline of her cheeks and chin. His firm fingers were cool and his touch soft. She remembered the feel of Mr. Hodge's brittle fingers upon her wrist and the touch of his wet lips against her cheek. She had felt revulsion then. Was this strange sensation, which weighted her limbs and quickened her pulses, also revulsion?

For a brief moment Lord Danewood's hands stretched out to wind one of her curls around his finger. "What colour?" he murmured.

"As I told you, my lord, her hair is a dark chestnut brown," answered Madam Portunio with evident pride.

Lord Danewood rested his hands on the arm of his chair.

"You may pack your bags, Miss Barclay, I am taking you with me tonight. I have decided to offer you employment in my household."

Elizabeth started to protest that she had no wish whatsoever to work in Lord Danewood's house. She could not voice her dissent, however, because Madam Portunio burst into a shrill cry of anger. "We didn't agree that she should leave here!" she exclaimed. Remembering the huge sums of money that had already been mentioned, she added hastily, "My lord, I expected her to remain in my House."

"You may certainly have her back eventually," Lord Danewood said indifferently. "I doubt if I shall require her services for very long."

Madam Portunio pursed her lips angrily. She had expected to keep Miss Barclay under her control, and she was less than happy about losing sight of such a delectable piece of merchandise. "Well, my lord, I don't know that I wish to conclude the sale. This is a very valuable property that we're talking about."

Lord Danewood gestured impatiently. "My servant has come prepared with a banker's draft. He will be happy to discuss the terms of the transaction with you, and to re-negotiate some of the details if that seems necessary." He did not wait for Madam Portunio's response, but simply assumed her agreement. "We need a maid to pack Miss Barclay's belongings," he said. "I think that would be the most efficient way of speeding our departure."

Madam Portunio took a quick decision. Lord

Danewood might be blind, but he didn't seem a good prospect for cheating. Her capitulation was unexpectedly complete. With five hundred pounds at stake she had no real desire to quibble over Elizabeth's temporary place of residence. She smiled at Lord Danewood just as if their little disagreement had never occurred. "I'll find a maid to pack Miss Barclay's belongings and then I'll talk to your servant," she said sweetly.

Elizabeth was left staring angrily at Lord Danewood. She hardly knew where to begin her protests because she could not understand the strange financial transaction that had just occurred.

Leaving aside such puzzles, she had no wish to accompany a man whom she found cold and unfeeling. She drew herself up very straight so that she could look directly at Lord Danewood, even though she knew he could not see her.

"I am not seeking permanent employment, my lord," she said. "I have no wish to leave Madam Portunio. I have only just arrived here in London and I did not expect to move so soon."

"You are being irrational," said Lord Danewood impatiently. "I may be blind, but I can't be less acceptable to you than some of the Old Devil's other clients. And I will see to it that you are well provided for when I dismiss you."

"What job do you have in mind, my lord, that you are already so certain I shall be dismissed? I have been tolerably well-educated and might prove to be more than satisfactory."

Lord Danewood gave a short laugh, utterly lacking in mirth. "I prefer to leave the precise nature of your duties undisclosed until I have had more time to consider the matter," he said. "Your voice and behaviour seem acceptable, and I daresay you've been well-trained in mimicking the manners of a lady. But I need to explore the ramifications further before reaching a final decision. You don't have to worry. Whatever I decide in the end, you will not suffer for coming with me."

"But it isn't respectable for a young woman to accept a job without first finding out the precise nature of her duties," said Elizabeth. "Surely it would be more proper for Lady Danewood, your wife, to decide whether or not I am suited for the work you have in mind?"

Lord Danewood gave every appearance of one struck dumb from astonishment. When finally he spoke, his face was wreathed in amusement. "Your jest is...diverting...Miss Barclay. But you will be relieved to hear that I have no wife."

"No wife!" Elizabeth was horrified to discover that Lord Danewood expected her to go and live in a bachelor household. "No wife!" she repeated. "But I cannot work in a house which has no mistress," she said. "You must tell me what you expect me to do, my lord!"

Madam Portunio re-entered the room before Lord Danewood could reply to her protests. Her beaming smile was once more firmly in place and Elizabeth needed no second glance to see that she would receive no support from her current employer. She had thought from the first that Madam Portunio's smiles bore little relationship to the warmth of Madam Portunio's heart. She was too perceptive to deny the obvious truth in front of her: Lord Danewood's draft had been large enough to purchase for him all the smiles which had previously been lavished upon Elizabeth.

A bulky-looking man, presumably Lord Danewood's servant, walked over to his master's chair. "Everything has been settled in accordance with your instructions, my lord. The girl's belongings have been taken out to the carriage. May I escort you to the door?"

"Your disapproval is showing, Sam," said Lord Danewood, and Elizabeth was astonished to hear the warmth of affectionate laughter that bubbled at the back of his voice. Lord Danewood stood up and inclined his head in Madam Portunio's direction. Despite his blindness, he seemed to have an uncanny capacity for sensing where people stood. "Thank you for your assistance. Perhaps you will see that Miss Barclay is provided with a reliable escort to my carriage?"

"Peterson shall take her," said Madam Portunio. "Don't worry, my lord, she'll have no chance to run away." She turned to Elizabeth, once again all smiles. "Good-bye, my dear. I am sure you will be very happy with his lordship, and I hope I may welcome you back to my little establishment at some time in the future."

"But I cannot go just like this! It's the middle of the night!" Panic invaded Elizabeth's whole mind. "That is to say...I don't have a pelisse, or an evening cloak to wear with this dress." It was not what she had intended to say, but her brain was numb with shock.

"Peterson shall give you a lovely new velvet cloak that I had made for myself." Lord Danewood's servant had paid Madam Portunio one hundred pounds over the agreed figure and she was prepared to be generous. After all, the girl possessed only two pathetic bundles of shabby clothes apart from the white evening gown she was wearing. Madam Portunio patted Elizabeth on the arm. "I daresay Lord Danewood will buy you as many pretty gowns as you wish." She tugged on the golden silk cords of a bellpull and Peterson arrived almost immediately.

"When you have escorted Lord Danewood and his servant to the door, please go to my rooms and fetch the blue velvet cape hanging in the wardrobe by the window." Madam Portunio gave another, even wider smile. "Give the cloak to Miss Barclay. She is leaving us already after such a short stay." Her glance was suddenly full of warning. "Make sure that she goes straight into Lord Danewood's coach once she has the cloak."

"Yes, ma'am." Peterson bowed stolidly, although his brain seethed as he escorted Lord Danewood to the front door. The Old Devil had obviously sold the girl for a better price than she'd expected. She looked like a hungry cat who'd just swallowed a dish of the very best cream. He hoped Danewood would prove a kind lover, since Peterson couldn't help feeling sympathetic towards the lovely Elizabeth Barclay. Did she have *any* idea what she'd let herself in for? Peterson sighed as he bowed to Lord Danewood and hurried back to fetch the cloak. He had three daughters of his own to get married off respectably and he had no time for allowing sentimentality to get in the way of business profit. He'd clawed his way out of the slums and into this profitable position and he wasn't going to throw away his daughters' future for the sake of a young woman with nothing to recommend her except a sweet smile and a soft voice.

"Here you are, Miss," he said gruffly as he

walked into Madam Portunio's parlour. "Here's your new cloak."

He could see that Elizabeth's violet eyes were filled with fear, so he turned away. Madam Portunio spoke sharply.

"Hurry up, then, Peterson. Take Miss Barclay to Lord Danewood's carriage. His horses have already been kept waiting far too long."

Peterson did not speak until Elizabeth was at the door of the carriage. "Good luck, Miss," he said still not meeting her eye. "I've always heard that he's a good sort of fellow."

He climbed sedately back up the stairs and the door of Madam Portunio's club slammed shut, leaving the carriage in a pool of darkness.

FIVE

Elizabeth curled as deeply into her corner of the barouche as she could manage. She hoped that Lord Danewood would not start to question her, although at the moment he appeared lost in thought and unlikely even to speak. If she had not known such a thing to be impossible, she would have said he had forgotten her presence.

She studied Lord Danewood's profile with covert interest. Even though she had already made up her mind to escape from him as soon as possible, she could not deny the fascination exerted by his austere features and the tantalising black spectacles. What colour were his eyes, she wondered?

As soon as she realized just where her thoughts were wandering, she tried to force her mind back to planning her escape, but she quickly gave up her useless efforts. It was impossible to make detailed plans before she had seen his house.

Despite all the turmoil of her short stay in London she felt that she had already learned one valuable lesson. In future she would need to be more careful about choosing her lodgings. Running away was not a habit she could afford to indulge for very long.

Unconsciously her hand moved to the precious pouch of coins, still tucked into the pockets of her petticoat. It was reassuring to hear the gentle chink of coin against coin, and her eyes filled with tears as she remembered her mother, risking her husband's anger in order to aid her daughter's escape.

"Counting your earnings, my dear?" Lord Danewood's sarcastic question jerked Elizabeth out of her nostalgic daydream.

"No, my lord," she replied shortly, "As Madam Portunio and I both informed you, I was not with her long enough to earn any payment."

"I remember what you both *said*." She could not mistake his satirical emphasis on the final word.

She started to make an indignant protest, resenting his implication that she might not always speak the truth, but the protest died on her lips. She was not telling outright lies, but she was guilty of lying by implication. Elizabeth stared wistfully at her hands. If life inside Barclay Manor had been boring, life outside it was proving unexpectedly complicated.

"Nothing to say, Miss Barclay?" Lord Danewood's voice, filled with mockery, emphasized her silence.

"I'm tired my lord. I am looking forward to retiring to my room and getting some rest."

"Even if you are exhausted, Miss Barclay,

surely you would expect most men to insist upon enjoying an immediate return upon their investment?"

She stared at him blankly. She was so tired of people who spoke in riddles. Did he want to keep her up talking about investments at this hour of the night? Or was he actually suggesting, as he seemed to be, that *she* was his investment? She knew that he had given money to Madam Portunio, and for a moment blind panic gripped the muscles of her stomach. Slavery had been abolished in the British Empire, but could he possibly mean that she had been *bought*?

"I cannot begin to imagine what you wish to imply, my lord." She tried to sound firm, although she felt sure he would detect the quiver lurking at the back of her voice. "It is too late at night to start solving riddles."

"You need not bother to protest, my dear. My plans for you do not include night-time visitations. As yet."

The carriage jerked to an abrupt halt, precluding the necessity for any reply, which was fortunate since Elizabeth once again had no idea what to say. The coachman opened the door of the carriage and waited courteously for Elizabeth to alight. As soon as she was on the pavement she turned to offer assistance to Lord Danewood. Disagreeable he might be, but he was also blind and Elizabeth could not repress her sympathy for his plight.

Lord Danewood reached out his hand and encountered the smooth kid of Elizabeth's gloved fingers instead of the sturdy arm of the coachman.

"Will you permit me to guide you, my lord?"

Her voice was gentle. Lord Danewood had made little reference to his blindness but she suspected that the loss of his sight was a recent occurrence and one, moreover, to which he was far from reconciled.

"My coachman is perfectly capable of directing me," said Lord Danewood curtly.

She accepted the snub without protest and followed her employer—her would-be employer, she corrected herself—up the shallow flight of steps to his front door.

It was a massive entrance, painted ebony black and flanked by marble-clad pillars. The door swung open as soon as they reached the top step and they were greeted by a middle-aged woman, soberly clad and stern of face. Fortunately for her peace of mind, Elizabeth was too fatigued to start wondering why an aristocrat of Lord Danewood's apparent means should choose to have his front door tended by a female servant. Anybody with the least pretension to gentility hired a butler precisely for this purpose. Apart from the housekeeper and Sam, there seemed to be no other servants in the massive house. Elizabeth decided they must all be in bed.

Lord Danewood made no effort to introduce her to the housekeeper, or to make her familiar with her surroundings. He simply halted abruptly in the middle of the long hall and spoke without turning to face her. "Goodnight, Miss Barclay. Mrs. Smithers will take you to your room."

He waited until Elizabeth had crossed the polished hallway and had joined the housekeeper at the bottom of the flight of stairs.

"Miss Barclay!" he called softly and for some

reason she shivered as he spoke her name. "If you should be contemplating running away, may I give you a piece of advice to ponder during the night? Do not make the attempt, Miss Barclay. I don't look favourably upon wasted investments and my investment in you, my dear, is substantial."

"I was simply looking forward to a good night's sleep, my lord." She was so angered by his arrogance of manner that she conveniently suppressed all memory of her decision to run away.

"Then I take it I shall have the pleasure of interviewing you in my bookroom at ten o'clock tomorrow morning." Lord Danewood did not bother to conceal the irony of his words. "Mrs. Smithers will help you to see that you keep the appointment promptly."

"Yes, I'll do that, my lord." Mrs. Smithers' voice did not live up to the cosiness of her appearance. It was as flat and cold as her master's. "If you will follow me, Miss, I'll show you to your room."

Elizabeth woke up when sunlight filtered through a crack in the shutters. She lay still in the bed, listening to the sounds of iron-clad carriage wheels rolling across cobbled streets. A glance at her watch told her that it was past nine o'clock and she was amazed to find that she had slept through the noisy hours of the early morning. Just as she started to get out of bed there was a brief knock at the door, and Mrs. Smithers entered the bedroom.

"I've brought you some tea, Miss, and some water for washing. Best hurry. The master doesn't like to be kept waiting."

She left the room without bothering to find out

if Elizabeth had any comments to make about these instructions.

Elizabeth, in any case, had nothing to say. She was overcome by the luxury of eating breakfast in her room. She sipped the hot tea and crunched a piece of toast, marvelling at the generous portions of food that were served both here and in Madam Portunio's household. She ate quickly, then crossed to the marble washstand where Mrs. Smithers had left the painted china jug, filled with water. Steam still rose from the hot, scented water, and she thought to herself how lucky Londoners seemed to be. She knew that she ought not to stay in Lord Danewood's house but, as she discovered the joys of washing without almost freezing, she allowed herself to hope that her eventual employer would be a Londoner shaped in the same extravagant mould as Madam Portunio and Lord Danewood.

When she was washed and dressed in her best black bodice and woollen skirt, she sat down in front of the large mirror to do her hair. She administered a hundred strokes as Mama had taught her and then, in a gesture of defiance towards the absent Sir William, looped the curls into a soft chestnut coil at the nape of her neck. She added her best white lace collar and cuffs to the sober black outfit and she felt a burst of confidence when she glanced into the mirrors. She knew so little of fashion that she decided she looked quite dashing. The people at Barclay Manor would scarcely recognize this creature with the shining eyes and softly-curling hair.

She had no opportunity to ask herself why her appearance had suddenly become a matter of such importance, because Mrs. Smithers appeared in the bedroom just as she was giving the last twitch to her skirts.

"Will you come with me, Miss?" she asked, her manner indicating that Elizabeth had no choice in the matter. "His lordship doesn't like to be kept hanging about."

She followed Mrs. Smithers down the stairs, so lost in thought that she forgot to pay any attention to the layout of the house. She chided herself angrily when the housekeeper halted and knocked on the panels of the study door. How was she going to find a way of escape when she kept allowing her attention to wander?

"Enter!" Lord Danewood's curt command added a fresh spur to her anger. She hadn't escaped from one tyrant in Barclay Manor simply to fall into the hands of another in London.

She marched into the study in a rebellious frame of mind but stood still when she saw Lord Danewood. He was leaning by a mullioned window overlooking the small garden. His eyes, masked by dark-tinted spectacles, stared unseeingly across the empty flower-beds and smooth-cut grass. A mass of daffodils, braving the March wind, made a splash of turbulent colour in a far corner of the garden. Elizabeth, looking at the flowers, forgot all the reasons why she ought to dislike Lord Danewood and felt her heart lurch in sympathy for all he had lost.

"The daffodils are very beautiful, my lord. Have your gardeners told you they are in full bloom?" She didn't know herself why she wanted to share that dancing splash of colour with him.

He turned slowly away from the window and

she divined the inexplicable wave of shock that seemed to go through him as he turned. His dark glasses made an impenetrable barrier in front of his eyes, but in the bright morning light she could see, as she hadn't seen the previous night, that his face was pale and that lines of strain were etched around his nose and mouth.

He ignored her comment about the flowers. "I trust you slept well, Miss Barclay?" He didn't wait for her to reply. "You may sit down if you wish. I prefer to remain standing."

She sank into a nearby chair. It was easier to sit than to stand up, when his chilly voice caused her legs to tremble with unpleasant memories of similar encounters with her father. "Why did you come to London, Miss Barclay?" he asked with an abruptness that shattered the remnants of her composure. "Why have you left the protection of your family?"

She had already decided to keep her answers brief. That way there was less chance of getting tangled up in her own lies. "My mother could no longer support me at home, my lord, so I left to find employment in the capital city." That, at least, was almost true.

"Does your mother know the nature of your current employment? Did she know of your stay in Madam Portunio's House?"

"No, indeed not, my lord." This time there was no mistaking the fervent sincerity of her response. "My family wouldn't approve of gambling and other such forms of profligate entertainment."

Lord Danewood gave a brief, cold smile. "The ring of sincerity at last. Perhaps, after all, Madam Portunio was not lying when she claimed you were

75

fresh up from the country." It seemed to Elizabeth that Lord Danewood stared at her, as if willing his blind eyes to see. "How on earth did you end up in her House?"

"It was recommended to me," said Elizabeth stiffly. "And if you please, my lord, I should prefer to discuss the details of the job you have for me, rather than the details of my past."

"That I can well believe." Again he did not attempt to conceal his disdain. "Tell me, Miss Barclay, have you attended school? Do you have all the usual female accomplishments?"

"I was instructed chiefly by my mother. She tried very hard but I don't think I have much natural talent for water-colours and playing the pianoforte."

"Your talents undoubtedly lie in other directions." Lord Danewood sat down suddenly at his desk. It occurred to Elizabeth as she watched his swift movements that he must once have been a very energetic and athletic man.

"Miss Barclay, I want to be quite sure there has been no misunderstanding. You sound to me as though you are everything Madam Portunio claimed: young, innocent, educated and definitely a lady. Are you *sure* you knew precisely what was involved in your terms of employment with Madam Portunio?"

"Naturally I knew what was involved. How could I accept a job without first discussing the terms of my employment? Madam Portunio explained most fully what I would be expected to do and what the gentlemen, her clients, would expect."

"Let us speak quite frankly, Miss Barclay. Did

you feel no scruples about working in such a place?"

"I have my living to earn," she said icily. "We cannot always be as nice as we would wish in our choice of occupation."

While she was speaking, Lord Danewood apparently reached a decision. He ceased to juggle with the steel pens laid out on his desk and stood up with renewed decisiveness.

"Far be it from me, Miss Barclay, to instil in you scruples that you appear to lack. Your profession makes you a convenient tool for my purpose and a tool, moreover, that I can use without qualm. I had almost despaired of finding somebody capable of projecting your aura of gentility. Madam Portunio's was by no means the first establishment I had visited in the course of my search. And I have lost count of the number of actresses I have interviewed."

"Actresses!" Elizabeth interjected in horrified accents. "I cannot think I should be suited to any job which required an actress, my lord." It was bad enough that she had broken every family rule and engaged in paid employment at a private club. To appear upon the *public* stage was unthinkable, even though she had already broken so many of the rules.

Lord Danewood turned at the sound of her outraged voice, then laughed with reluctant amusement. "You really are the oddest creature," he said, his voice warmed by laughter. "But there is no cause for alarm. I wish you to play out your part upon a very small stage. In fact, you are to accompany me to my home in the country."

"Oh," said Elizabeth, feeling disappointed to be

leaving London, until she remembered that of course she was only pretending to accept this mysterious job. She smiled brightly, anxious to forestall any of Lord Danewood's lingering suspicions. She didn't want the servants to receive orders to keep the outer doors of the house permanently locked. "Well," she said, doing her best to sound cheerful. "It will be pleasant to spend the spring in the country. Where is your home, my lord?"

"In Berkshire," he said shortly, and Elizabeth was glad that he could not see her dismayed expression. Thank goodness she didn't really have to take this job. Of all the counties in England, how unfortunate that he should come from the same one as her own family! She was so preoccupied with her own worries that she didn't notice Lord Danewood had lost some of his self-assurance.

"I am going to have to trust you with a certain amount of personal information," said Lord Danewood at last. "I am reluctant to do this, for obvious reasons, and one of my requirements for offering you this job is that you should agree to leave the country once your period of employment with me is at an end. Is this acceptable to you?"

Elizabeth bristled with indignation. "Most certainly not!" she said before remembering that she was supposed to agree with everything he said. She corrected herself hastily. "That is to say, my lord, I cannot imagine why it would be necessary to leave England. Where should I go and how would I support myself away from my native land?"

"Ah," said Lord Danewood with cynical satisfaction. "I am glad that we arrived so swiftly at the hub of the matter. You will be gratified to learn that I plan to advance you one thousand pounds when your work with me is satisfactorily completed."

"A thousand pounds!" exclaimed Elizabeth with all the astonishment he could possibly have hoped for. She wondered if everybody in London threw money around in this extraordinary fashion. First Madam Portunio offered her two pounds a month for serving tea and smiling at a few gentlemen. Now Lord Danewood was offering her a thousand pounds for...Her thoughts trailed into uncertainty. "A thousand pounds for what, my lord?"

"First I must have your promise," said Lord Danewood. "You may go to Europe, or Canada if you prefer to hear English spoken. You could even go to the United States if you have a fancy to observe the rule of the masses."

Elizabeth forgot that this interview was all part of a charade and that she would be leaving Lord Danewood before nightfall. "Do you mean that I could travel to Italy, to Rome or Athens? Somewhere like that?"

"If you wish. Although I would imagine Paris is more in your line. What would a young woman such as yourself find to do in Athens, or Rome?"

"I could study the Classical ruins," said Elizabeth with great dignity. "It has been a particular wish of mine to inspect the antiquities of Rome ever since I first read Mr. Gibbon's *Decline and Fall of the Roman Empire*."

"But naturally," he said. "I wonder that such a reason did not occur to me, given the nature of the establishment where we met." He made a sudden gesture of irritation with his hands. "To return to the matter at issue between us. I take it we're agreed that you will leave England once your work with me is over?"

Elizabeth folded her hands meekly in her lap. "Yes, my lord." Since she had no intention of starting work for Lord Danewood, her answer was not exactly a lie. "But you still haven't told me what I am to do for you."

"You have probably wondered how I came to lose my sight," he said. "You may have guessed that it was a recent occurrence. There was a fire in the stables of Danewood Hall and I was knocked unconscious by one of the panicked horses. I was found by my groom on the floor of the tackroom and dragged to safety just before the entire stable-block went up in flames." His mouth twisted into a bitterly derisive smile. "My physicians assure me that I am fortunate not to have been more badly burned. My head was apparently protected from the flames by a heavy saddle which fell upon me. The saddle, however, seems to have dealt me a blow that affects the optic nerves, so I am not sure that I consider myself as fortunate as the doctors assure me I am."

Elizabeth looked at him with genuine sympathy. "It's even harder to bear misfortune when those around us won't accept that we are entitled to be miserable," she said. She understood instinctively that for a man of Lord Danewood's restless vitality, blindness must seem an intolerable burden.

"Is there no hope that your sight may return as suddenly as it left you, my lord?"

"I have discovered," said Lord Danewood dryly, "that there are few professionals more adept at hedging their bets than a group of doctors called in on consultation. You may take your pick of answers to that question, Miss Barclay. Choose your physician or surgeon and you can hear whatever answer you wish."

"Then you mustn't lose hope," said Elizabeth.

"*I* have not lost hope," said Lord Danewood. "Those around me, however, seem less sanguine about my chances of returning to a normal way of life. And that, Miss Barclay, is in part why I have sought you out."

"How so, my lord?"

"At the time of the accident I was betrothed to Miss Clarissa Fanshawe, the daughter of a neighbor, the Honourable Henry Fanshawe." He paused uncertainly. "I am still betrothed to Miss Fanshawe, but she would prefer to be released from her engagement. She has made it clear to me in a hundred different ways that she abhors the thought of marriage to somebody who is blind. I have offered several times to release her from her commitment to me and I know that she wants to be free. Her parents, however, will not permit us to break the engagement. The Honourable Henry is in financial distress and his circumstances don't permit Clarissa to turn her back on such a splendid match as I, merely because she has become squeamish at the thought of marrying a man who is blind."

"I see," Elizabeth said, torn between disgust with the fickle Miss Fanshawe and sympathy for a fellow-sufferer. After all, she knew only too well what it meant to be brow-beaten by an unfeeling parent.

"Do you see?" asked Lord Danewood. "Somehow

I doubt if Clarissa's sensitivities can be understood by somebody who hasn't experienced them at first hand." Almost to himself he muttered, "I should never have suspected her true nature had it not been for my accident."

"But you have some sort of plan to free yourself from this commitment?" Elizabeth asked.

Lord Danewood allowed a slight smile to twist his mouth. "Oh yes! I have a plan. I left Danewood five weeks ago, announcing that I was seeking treatment from the London specialists. I plan to return from London with a bride. If I'm already married, I can't be expected to honour my proposals to Clarissa."

"I don't think that's very fair on your new bride, my lord. There will be a shocking scandal and your unfortunate bride will be at the centre of the storm. Just imagine how uncomfortable it will be for a young lady to find herself in a new home, and shunned by all your neighbours!"

"Very true, Miss Barclay. But I have made sure that my bride-to-be is less sensitive than most young ladies. In fact, I have decided that my bride cannot be a lady at all. You see, Miss Barclay, I plan to return to Danewood with a 'bride', but I don't intend to complete the formality of a wedding ceremony."

Elizabeth wrinkled her brow in puzzlement. "If you don't have a wedding ceremony, my lord, you won't be married."

Lord Danewood smiled. "Precisely, Miss Barclay. In order to be free of Clarissa I need to be married, but I have no desire for a wife. With your quick wits, Miss Barclay, I'm sure you've deduced your prospective role in this affair. I wish *you* to be my bride. Without the formality of a marriage ceremony, of course."

Elizabeth stood up from the chair and clasped her hands in front of her. She was pleased to discover that her shaking knees supported her quite adequately. "Perhaps, my lord, you don't fully understand the extent of your insult. It would be charitable to think that the blow to your head has affected your judgment as well as your eyesight. How could you offer such an improper suggestion to a lady who finds herself alone and unprotected in your house? I must ask your permission to leave at once, my lord."

He turned to stare at Elizabeth. Even the dark glasses could not conceal the mingled irritation and bewilderment written on his face. "Come, Miss Barclay, let us not play childish games with one another. I consider my offer in the nature of a compliment to your excellent deportment. Where is the dishonour in taking you away from Madam Portunio's establishment and offering you a few months' employment in my own household? Indeed, it seems to me that I am placing a flattering degree of trust in your basic honesty and good-nature."

"I should not need to remind you, Lord Danewood, that a lady's honour is irretrievably compromised if she enters into...into the sort of arrangement you are suggesting."

Lord Danewood brought his fist down on to the desk with a heavy crash. "Damn it, woman! Are you suggesting that work at Madam Portunio's *enhances* a woman's honour?"

Elizabeth's eyes flashed fire. "I don't expect to be shouted at, my lord, and blindness does not excuse a gentleman who utters profanities in the presence of a lady." She looked up and glimpsed Lord Danewood's exasperation and caught her breath before she could make any more rash speeches. What *was* she doing, arguing with Lord Danewood in this perverse fashion? She sat down on the chair again and tried to control the quiver of anger that lingered in her voice. She needed to lull his suspicions, not provoke his wrath.

"Perhaps it would be better if we didn't discuss my employment with Madam Portunio any further, my lord, since it seems to promote misunderstandings between us. But I don't like the idea of playing the role of your wife, my lord, so I should prefer to collect my belongings and leave here, if you please."

"It has been difficult to find somebody suitable for the role, Miss Barclay, and I don't think you have taken the time to consider all the advantages. May I remind you once again of the thousand pounds that will be yours once this little pantomime has achieved its purpose?"

She pretended to consider his offer. "A thousand pounds is a great deal of money. Perhaps, once I am used to the idea, I wouldn't find it impossible to play the part of your wife."

His smile was entirely cynical. "I'm relieved that you have so quickly come round to my way of thinking, Miss Barclay. Since we neither of us want this make-believe marriage to last very long, would you like to hear the plans I have made for ending it?"

"Yes, please." She did her best to sound enthusiastic. The sooner this interview ended, the sooner she could start planning her escape.

"As soon as the situation with Miss Fanshawe has been cleared up, we'll leave together for a delayed honeymoon. We'll go to Rome, Athens, wherever you wish. While we're there, you'll be struck down by a tragic fever and I shall return to Berkshire alone, a grieving widower."

"And what of me, my lord?"

He shrugged. "You will be left, a thousand pounds richer, in whatever city you have chosen. If we have spent a few weeks on holiday there together, you will have time to establish yourself in the local community. And I shall be able to add accurate details to my sad account of our final days together."

Elizabeth swallowed hard. She suspected that he wasn't telling her the truth. It didn't matter, of course, because she wanted no part of his schemes, but she guessed that he would be a dangerous man to deceive. She knew her voice sounded breathless when she finally spoke, but she trembled to contemplate the consequences if Lord Danewood discovered she was deliberately tricking him. She did her best to look like a woman who was only interested in money.

"Very well, my lord. I'll do as you ask and accompany you into Berkshire as your wife." With a touch of cunning she hadn't suspected she possessed, she pressed him for guarantees about the money he had promised. "How do I know you'll keep your word and pay me a thousand pounds?"

Lord Danewood walked over to the fireplace and tugged at a heavy bellpull. "While you remain with me, I'll give you five guineas each week as evidence of my good faith. I doubt if you could earn that much anywhere else, so you won't be losing anything. The balance of the money will be paid to you when we part company." He smiled, although she could detect no mirth in the tautly-stretched lips. "You'll have to trust me to a certain extent, Miss Barclay. Just as I will have to trust you. To a certain extent."

There was a tap at the door and at Lord Danewood's word of command, the housekeeper entered the study. She waited just inside the door and Lord Danewood's darkly-screened eyes turned in her direction. Elizabeth was struck again by the power which emanated from this blinded man.

"What is Miss Barclay wearing, Mrs. Smithers?"

The housekeeper gave no sign that she found the question strange. "A black skirt and silk bodice, my lord. White lace collar and cuffs. Good lace, but the skirt's shockingly out of style."

"You will arrange for the dressmaker this afternoon, Mrs. Smithers. A travelling suit, three morning dresses, two afternoon gowns and a selection of dinner dresses. I need not remind you that the dressmaker must be skilful, but not one who is patronised by the fashionable matrons of London society."

"No, my lord, you don't have to remind me." Mrs. Smithers smoothed her hands over her neat black apron. "Bedgowns will be needed, my lord and various other items of a similar nature if the maids at the Hall are to be kept from gossiping."

Lord Danewood turned his unseeing gaze away from Mrs. Smithers and towards Elizabeth. His mouth had once again relaxed into the faintest suggestion of humour.

"God knows, we cannot have the Danewood

maids discussing Miss Barclay's lack of bedgowns. Perhaps you would be good enough to purchase the necessary items in a suitably frivolous style?"

"Yes, my lord. Shall I take Miss Barclay back to her room now?"

"Very well," said Lord Danewood. "I shall expect to see Miss Barclay again tomorrow morning, so that I can start instructing her in some of the matters she will need to know before arriving at Danewood."

Mrs. Smithers did not look at Elizabeth when she spoke to her. "Would you follow me, Miss? I would like to serve you luncheon before the dressmaker arrives."

Elizabeth started to protest and then gave up the attempt. There was no reason to insist upon clarifying matters with Lord Danewood when she planned to be out of the house within the next few minutes. She smiled sweetly at Lord Danewood, forgetting that he could not see this sign of her docility.

"I look forward to our next meeting, my lord," she said and followed Mrs. Smithers from the room.

The housekeeper, who had already shown herself to be a woman of few words, conducted Elizabeth up the narrow staircase in silence. The layout of the house was more complex than Elizabeth had imagined and she could not see any exit other than through the main hall. Mrs. Smithers was already opening the door to Elizabeth's bedroom.

"Your lunch will be brought up in a few minutes, Miss," she said. "I don't doubt the dressmaker will be arriving shortly. Will there be anything else, Miss?"

"No thank you." Elizabeth smiled cheerfully, as if life could hold out no more interesting prospect than a quiet lunch, followed by a session with the dressmaker. Inwardly she worried at the short time available for making her escape. How long would it be between Mrs. Smithers' arrival with the lunch and the appearance of the dressmaker? She smiled again, swallowing her nerves as well as she could. "It seems to me I have only just finished eating breakfast and already you're saying it's lunch time."

"There's no reason for you to feel hungry, Miss. Lord Danewood wouldn't want that." Mrs. Smithers failed to respond to Elizabeth's smiles and walked briskly from the room. There was a click and a slight pause before her firm footsteps faded away.

Elizabeth guessed the significance of the click as soon as she heard it and dashed to the door, tugging on its delicate china knob, then beating her fists against the solid mahogany panels. Her actions had no effect, other than to bruise her fingers, because the door was firmly locked.

She flew to the window, pushing aside the thick lace curtains that obscured her view of the outside world. The glass panes were barred with highly-functional iron bands. Despairingly she tested the unyielding bars. The iron was so new it had not even begun to rust.

She plumped down on the bed because her legs were suddenly too weak to support her. So much for her naive intention to escape! Her flight from Barclay Manor had only led her to this. She was locked in a luxurious prison contrived by a blind nobleman of doubtful sanity and even more dubious morals!

She was too frightened for tears and certainly too frightened for calm planning. She tried to comfort herself with the thought that Lord Danewood obviously intended to feed and clothe her, which did not seem the actions of a madman bent upon death and destruction. Elizabeth's imagination, severely hampered by a lack of information about the basic facts of nature, began to run riot through the various fates that might be in store for her. Even she could no longer believe that Lord Danewood was going to all this trouble just to have an excuse for terminating his betrothal.

After fifteen minutes of increasingly hysterical worrying, she decided to sit down in the chair by the fire and wait for lunch.

There didn't seem to be much else that she could do.

SIX

Elizabeth's plans for escape were never realised.
Lord Danewood's travelling carriage was brought
round to the front door five weeks after her flight
from Barclay Manor and with the arrival of the
carriage, her last hope of freedom vanished. Mrs.
Smithers and Sam, the groom, escorted her out of
the house, each holding firmly on to one of Elizabeth's arms. She had a brief glimpse of the busy
London street before she was locked inside the
carriage with only Lord Danewood for company.

She was determined not to talk to her employer—gaoler would have been a more accurate
title, she thought angrily—so there was nothing
she could do except stare out of the carriage window, her chin thrust outwards in a gesture of defiance. She pondered the disagreeable fact that
during five whole weeks she had never once come
close to making good her escape from Lord Dane-

wood's clutches. She closed her mind to the suggestion thrust forward by her tiresomely active conscience, that if she had tried a little harder, she would have been more likely to succeed.

During her captivity, the major part of each day had been consumed in sessions with the dressmaker, a stout woman whose own unfashionable garments gave no hint of the masterly outfits she was able to create. Elizabeth allowed her fingers to rub gently against the cashmere of her new grey travelling suit. She couldn't disguise the pleasure she derived from watching the soft folds settle over the hoops of her crinoline, even though she shuddered at the impropriety of allowing Lord Danewood to buy her clothes.

The carriage stopped for a moment at a busy crossing and Elizabeth watched a young muffinseller hawk his wares along the street. She was scarcely aware of the scene before her eyes as she re-lived the frustrations of the past few weeks. When she had not been busy with the dressmaker, Mrs. Smithers, Sam and Lord Danewood had conspired to see that she was never alone. If she retired to her bedroom, the door was locked. If she suggested a walk, the groom would take her into the tiny back garden. Her requests to explore London were politely rejected, although she was driven out occasionally in the carriage.

The constant supervision was exercised subtly at first, but when Elizabeth protested at her state of captivity, Lord Danewood abandoned the pretence of freedom. She was well-treated and courteously attended. Nevertheless, there was no longer any concealment of the fact that she was a prisoner in his house.

On her first Sunday in captivity she had asked for permission to attend a church service. Lord Danewood denied her request with a curt shake of the head. "I can't allow it," he said when she repeated her plea. "We couldn't supervise you properly in a Church and there is no time now to find a substitute. You are perfect for the role and I need your services. I still hope to acquire them willingly—you must admit that I'm paying you generously—but I will force your co-operation if that becomes necessary."

Goaded beyond prudence, she had burst into an impassioned protest. "How do you know that I won't destroy your whole plan once we arrive at Danewood Hall? What is to stop me telling Clarissa Fanshawe that we are not really married and that my presence is merely a trick to deceive her?"

His face betrayed that he was startled by her words, as if he had not thought of such an eventuality in all his clever planning. There was no hint of uncertainty in his voice, however, when he did finally speak.

"I think you will be wise enough to refrain from doing something so foolish, Miss Barclay. After all, if you do as I bid you, you will stand to profit considerably. What possible reason could you have for ruining my plans when no benefit would accrue to you? Be reasonable, Miss Barclay. For some reason you have taken me in dislike, but I'm offering you a comfortable home and the chance of an excellent nest-egg. Madam Portunio could never have offered you as much. Why persist in trying to thwart me at every turn?"

When Lord Danewood spoke to her in this soothing fashion, Elizabeth found herself lulled into temporary acceptance of her lot. She allowed herself to daydream about starting a school somewhere in Italy and she reminded herself that, even if she escaped from Lord Danewood, she could never go back to her family. Her father would have no more interest in her, except to disown her publicly. When her reflections became too gloomy, she consoled herself with the thought that at least there was no longer any danger of Mr. Hodge wanting to marry her.

Despite her occasional daydreams, Elizabeth was wise enough to know that Lord Danewood was lying to her. She had little experience of the world, but her commonsense warned her that his preparations were too meticulous for a man who merely wished to rid himself of an inconvenient fiancée.

She tried from time to time to discover what his real reasons for acquiring a 'bride' might be, but she always came up against an impenetrable wall of silence. Lord Danewood was full of information about his days at school, his years of military service and the history of Danewood Hall. But his stories, vivid as they were, gave no hint of any real reason he might have for setting-up such an elaborate subterfuge.

"You are very silent, Elizabeth."

His voice broke into the turmoil of her thoughts, and she turned away from the carriage windows. He smiled slightly, and she knew that he had sensed how surprised she was to hear her Christian name on his lips.

"I can hardly continue to address you as 'Miss Barclay' now that we are married—more or less. My name, by the way, is Roderick."

"My lord." He scowled at her and Elizabeth corrected herself with evident reluctance. "Roderick, can't you see how impossible this whole scheme is? We don't behave as a man and his wife. There is no comfortable air of intimacy between us."

Lord Danewood, his eyes covered by a black-silk bandage, turned in the direction of Elizabeth's voice. "I wager that at the end of a few weeks in Danewood Hall you will have forgotten that we are not actually married."

Elizabeth was no longer sure enough of herself to take him up on his wager. She was beginning to feel a bit afraid of the way she had adapted to her new life. Above all, she worried over the way in which her heartbeat quickened and the day seemed more sparkling as soon as Lord Danewood walked into the room. She tried to sound firmer than she felt when she replied.

"You can't possibly expect this charade to continue for very long. Surely it won't take more then twenty-four hours for the news of your marriage to travel to the Fanshawes."

"That's true," he said smoothly. "But I can't allow our marriage to end too quickly. I can't become a grieving widower until the Fanshawes have had time to settle their daughter's affairs. I should like to see Clarissa safely married off before you succumb to your tragic fever. I don't want to run the risk of a renewed betrothal."

Elizabeth tugged angrily at one of the carriage straps, wishing it might be a lock of Lord Danewood's luxuriant brown hair. "Heaven forbid that you should find yourself obliged to honour your commitments to Miss Fanshawe! I can see how inconvenient it would be if you became a widower before Miss Fanshawe was safely married off."

"Most inconvenient," he agreed with aggravating placidity. "I have no wish to be saddled with a reluctant bride who shudders every time her gaze turns in the direction of my eyes. Since you are determined to be cross with me, shall we turn the subject away from my wicked treatment of Miss Fanshawe? Would you care to go over once more the story we are going to tell upon our arrival at Danewood Hall?"

Elizabeth drew her gaze back from the passing hedgerows, green now with the freshness of late spring. She realised that this was her last opportunity to tell Lord Danewood the truth about her background. The carriage was travelling towards Reading, she had seen the signposts. She had only to tell him that she was the daughter of Sir William Barclay and she knew instinctively that he would drive her straight back to the Manor. Lord Danewood would have no room in his schemes for the gently-bred daughter of one of his distant neighbours.

She stared unseeingly at her grey kid gloves, newly purchased to match her travelling suit. Did she really want to be taken back to Barclay Manor, whatever fate might lie in wait for her at Danewood Hall? She sighed as she finally acknowledged to herself that she had enjoyed the weeks she had just spent with Lord Danewood. Despite the restrictions placed upon her movements, she had in many ways been freer in his house than she would have been in Barclay Manor. Her brief taste of liberty had only whetted her appetite for more.

Her upbringing had given her little practice in the useful art of self-deception. When she eventually brought her gaze level with Lord Danewood's bandaged eyes, she had already admitted to herself that she was going to Danewood Hall because she wanted to. She did not try to pretend that Lord Danewood had the power to force her consent, nor did she allow herself to pretend that escape was impossible. The house in London had been guarded, but as Lord Danewood's supposed wife she would have complete freedom once they arrived at Danewood Hall. Quite simply, she was accompanying Lord Danewood because she felt more alive in his company than she had ever done before.

"Elizabeth?" Lord Danewood's voice broke into her thoughts. "Was my question so very difficult to answer?"

"No, my lord. It wasn't difficult to answer. I was merely thinking. Would you like me to repeat for you the story you have made up to account for our hasty marriage?"

Lord Danewood shifted on the padded leather seat of the coach and a stray beam of sunlight highlighted the sudden pallor of his cheeks. "My lord," said Elizabeth, moving quite unconsciously to take one of his hands within her clasp. "My lord, do you feel unwell?"

"It is nothing." His voice was as light and even as before, although Elizabeth could now see that a thin film of sweat glistened on his forehead. "I am subject to headaches since my accident and I find the motion of the carriage particularly trying."

"Let me ask the coachman to stop for a while," said Elizabeth. She was alarmed by the pallor of his complexion and suspected from the deep lines etched between his nostrils and his mouth that the pain he suffered was considerable.

"No." His voice was harsh and Elizabeth could see that he was struggling to hide the weakness he felt. "Tell me how we are supposed to have met and fallen in love. It will be like hearing a bedtime story for young children."

She became conscious of the fact that she was still holding Lord Danewood's hand. She returned quickly to her other side of the carriage, rearranging the folds of her travelling suit so that it completely covered her toes. She immediately felt more composed, although Lord Danewood would not have been able to see even if her entire ankle had been exposed. She cleared her throat self-consciously.

"We met for the first time just after Christmas. You had left Danewood and travelled to London to visit some doctors. We were introduced to each other by a business associate at a small party and we fell immediately in love. We knew that it was an unequal match, and that you were promised elsewhere, but we could not help ourselves. I am the daughter of a wealthy merchant who lived in Liverpool."

"Very good," said Lord Danewood. "Nobody living in Berkshire knows the first thing about Liverpool, so your own ignorance will pass quite unnoticed. What was your father's occupation?"

"He owned several large drapery stores," said Elizabeth. "But he is now dead."

"Excellent. Everybody will be so embarrassed to think that I have rejected Clarissa Fanshawe in order to marry a shopkeeper's daughter that nobody will ask you for any details."

She was just as pleased as Lord Danewood to think that she was going to be able to gloss over all the circumstances of her background. "We married in February," she said. "But since the marriage was against the wishes of my family, the ceremony was a quiet one. We have been staying in London while we attempted to effect a reconciliation with the members of my family."

"Yes," he said with a sigh of satisfaction. "It all hangs together. If we can wait for another week or so, that will be long enough..."

"Long enough for what?"

He seemed startled by her question. "I didn't realise that I had spoken out loud. It's nothing important."

Elizabeth gripped her hands tightly together in her lap, as if by exerting pressure she could control the fright that caused her knees to quiver.

"I think, my lord, that it's past time for you to be honest with me. Your preparations are excessive for a man who wishes nothing more than to rid himself of an unwilling fiancée. I may be ignorant of city ways, but I am not a fool."

"That, my dear Elizabeth, becomes more evident with the passage of every hour we spend together." Lord Danewood lapsed into a short silence. "Can you not be content with the knowledge that I mean you no harm?" he asked at last. "I give you my word that what I have told you is the truth. Clarissa Fanshawe does not want to marry me and her parents are determined to force the match for purely financial reasons."

Elizabeth shook her head, forgetting that he

couldn't see her denial. "That is an insufficient reason, my lord. There are a dozen different excuses you could offer to Mr. Fanshawe. He may bluster and protest, but if you are adamant in your refusal, what can he do?"

"He can make life very difficult for Clarissa and for the man she really loves," said Lord Danewood reluctantly. "The present heir to Danewood is my cousin, David Vincent. David fell in love with Clarissa some months ago and she has now decided that she returns his feelings. They have many interests in common and would, I imagine, be ideally suited to one another."

"Is Mr. Fanshawe such an ogre that Clarissa can't tell him what she wants?" Elizabeth's question was not a sarcastic one. After all, she had needed to run away in order to avoid a forced marriage.

"Mr. Fanshawe can't afford to look with favour upon the match. David's income is sufficient for his needs but it cannot begin to compare with mine. Mr. Fanshawe needs money and Clarissa's personal happiness is a matter of little importance when set against her father's need for cash."

"I see," said Elizabeth. She knew only too well what it was like to be treated as little more than a pawn in some parental manoeuvre. But she did not allow her sympathy for Clarissa to overcome her judgment.

"Everything that you say may be true. But I'm not silly enough to believe that you scoured London looking for a make-believe bride just so that your cousin and Clarissa Fanshawe could get themselves married."

Lord Danewood moved his head in sudden pain.

"You are being paid to act out a role, Miss Barclay, not to think. Don't burden your pretty head with inappropriate thoughts. A thousand pounds is a great deal of money and should serve to stifle a great deal of curiosity."

He sank back against the squabs of the carriage and Elizabeth could see that his endurance was practically at an end. His pain, at least, was unfeigned and she was surprised at the degree of anxiety she felt. The coach gave a final sickening lurch and turned into one of the old posting inns, now rapidly disappearing in the face of increasing competition from the railways.

"Let me escort you into the inn, my lord. We shall both feel better for some refreshment. Trains may be dirty, but I think their motion is much more comfortable than this endless, rackety swaying." She bit her lip in vexation when she had spoken, annoyed with herself for pandering to Lord Danewood's weakness. Now was surely the moment to insist upon some answers to her questions, not to worry about the state of his health.

"Roderick," murmured Lord Danewood. "I am well known at this inn and in this district. You must remember to call me Roderick."

"Very well," said Elizabeth, sufficiently worried about his green complexion to have no interest in protesting.

Sam swung open the coach door, letting in a welcome breath of fresh, country air. Elizabeth smiled at the servant, quite forgetting how many times he had frustrated her efforts to escape. "Oh, it's good to smell flowers and fresh air again! I sometimes wondered if I should choke in all that London fog."

Lord Danewood stood on the carriage steps. "Do you smell flowers?" he asked. "How strange. I can smell nothing over the all-pervading odour of cattle-byres."

Elizabeth forgot that his answers to her questions had been so evasive and laughed with real amusement. "It seems you don't share my romantic nature, Roderick. How sad for you that where I smell the perfume of wild flowers, you are aware only of cows."

He placed his hand lightly upon her arm. "You will have to teach me to appreciate the flowers, my love. Who knows? Perhaps under your expert tutelage I, too, shall become a romantic. A life full of sunshine and bluebells. Is that what you are offering me, Elizabeth?"

She did not understand the thread of mockery that ran through his words, although she understood intuitively that the irony was directed inward towards himself rather than out towards her.

"That is only the beginning of what I have to offer you, my lor...Roderick." Elizabeth spoke almost at random, her mind full of feverish thoughts and apprehensions. "The welcoming party from the inn is approaching us, and they are looking at me with *great* curiosity."

Lord Danewood smiled, although she could detect the strain still lying behind his outward appearance of casual good humour. "I trust that you are ready to stand up to an onslaught of questions. This innkeeper is noted for his ale, not for his discretion. I think this will prove the first test of our story."

Elizabeth wondered if she should throw herself on the innkeeper's mercy and protest that she was being held against her will. Her eyes moved involuntarily to Lord Danewood's austere profile and she felt the pleas for help wither on her lips. "Never fear, my lord," she said, with a lingering trace of bitterness in her voice. She still didn't understand why she was aiding a man whom she could not trust. "You will find that you have hired the perfect wife."

He turned away from her. "That's what I am afraid of," he said.

"My lord," Sam interrupted hastily. "Mr. and Mrs. Cheam are almost within earshot."

Lord Danewood stood impassively while the innkeeper hurried up, bowing profusely. He waited while the man and his wife completed long and garbled speeches of welcome.

"Mr. and Mrs. Cheam," he said when they finally fell silent, and a curious smile hovered at the corner of his mouth. "I would like to present to you my wife, the Lady Danewood."

SEVEN

They arrived at Danewood Hall late in the afternoon. The carriage swung through a pair of massive, wrought-iron gates and bowled at a swift pace along the curved gravel driveway. Elizabeth peered out of the carriage window with a sinking heart, receiving a swift impression of vast gardens and an even larger expanse of ornamental parkland. Sycamore trees, grown to an immense height, lined the driveway. Their fresh spring leaves reflected the pale rays of the April sun and cast a green light on the path in front of the carriage.

Elizabeth, with the memory of her reception at the inn still uppermost in her mind, would have liked nothing better than to slip into her new home through an inconspicuous side-entrance. She felt she had already endured more than enough covert scrutiny and silent astonishment for one day. The steward, however, had other ideas about what was suitable for his supposed new mistress.

Alerted to his master's arrival by a message delivered from town the week before, he was determined to perform his job properly, even if Lord Danewood had so shockingly flouted the conventions. All the servants were hastily assembled, some in the courtyard, others in the Great Hall. The most humble clustered at the entrance to the kitchens, allowed to view their new mistress only from a respectful distance.

All of the servants, from the butler down to the youngest scullery-maid, stared at Elizabeth with open-mouthed curiosity. Years of training enabled them to execute the necessary bobs and bows. But even such superior domestics as these could not quite control their expressions. The supposed Lady Danewood's introduction was greeted with stares of mingled disapproval and amazement. For a few moments, looking along the ranks of hostile faces, Elizabeth actually envied Lord Danewood his blindness. At least it protected him from the most blatantly unfriendly stares.

It was a relief when he escorted her upstairs, sending various servants scurrying to fetch hot water and trays of refreshments. Lord Danewood of Danewood Hall was certainly a personage to be reckoned with. Elizabeth followed him upstairs with uncharacteristic meekness.

They arrived outside a large door with painted panels, and Lord Danewood bowed politely. "I shall look forward, my dear, to meeting you again at dinner."

"You aren't going to leave me alone?" Panic outran Elizabeth's sense of discretion.

He smiled and Elizabeth wondered if his servants could detect the warning in his smile as easily as she could. "My dear, even the most devoted of newly-weds must occasionally separate. I expect Janet has come upstairs with us. She shall stay and take care of your needs."

An elderly woman, with a red-cheeked country face, stepped forward from the cluster of maids and dipped into a small curtsey. "It'll be an honour to serve your ladyship," she said doubtfully. Her honest face was not well adapted to concealing subtle conflicts of emotion, and her expression flickered uneasily between natural friendliness and latent antagonism. The servants, Elizabeth decided, did not approve of their master's hasty marriage.

"And I shall be glad to have you as my maid, Janet." She answered the maid with as much friendliness as she could muster. She had lived with downtrodden servants in her father's house, and while she was supposed to be mistress of Danewood Hall the servants would be well treated.

Lord Danewood reached out for her hand, and when she placed her fingers within his clasp he raised them to his lips. He dropped a kiss on each of the gloved tips and she tried not to look flustered at this unexpected display of marital affection. Anxious to avoid looking directly at Lord Danewood, and equally anxious to avoid removing her hand from his grasp, she turned her gaze towards the coachman. Sam had shed his travelling coat and now stood discreetly by his master's side. He was evidently Lord Danewood's permanent guide and the only servant, as far as Elizabeth knew, who was aware of the true facts behind Lord Danewood's scandalous "marriage".

She pulled her hand away from Lord Danewood with sudden sharpness. It was impossible to keep up a convincing pretence of wifely affection in the face of Sam's knowing stare. "I plan to take a short rest now," she said trying to sound casual. "We shall meet at dinner."

Lord Danewood rested his hand on Sam's arm. "Wear your white evening gown, my dear. It will remind me of the delightful evening when we first met."

She was so outraged by his deliberate reference to their encounter at Madam Portunio's that she missed the significance of his request. It was not until several hours later, when she was almost ready to make her way downstairs for dinner, that she realised why his request had struck a jarring note. Who had told him that her evening gown had been white and why should he care whether or not she wore it again?

She gave a sudden gulp, worried by Lord Danewood's inexplicable knowledge, and whirled round just in time to observe Janet opening the door to her private sitting-room. Lord Danewood stood on the threshold, immaculately clad in formal evening clothes, his eyes shielded by dark glasses. He looked exactly as Elizabeth remembered him from that first terrifying encounter at Madam Portunio's.

"I have come to escort you downstairs, my dear. My cousin, David Vincent, is already waiting anxiously to meet you."

Elizabeth was not interested in her new "cousin".

"How do you like my dress?" she asked breathlessly.

He tilted his head to one side. "You will have to move, my dear. If you remain still I cannot hear that entrancing rustle I remember so well."

"Oh." Elizabeth let her breath come out in a tiny sigh. She scarcely knew what suspicions she had been harbouring, but Lord Danewood's innocent manner disarmed her anger and left her feeling a little foolish. Why shouldn't he have asked Sam the colour of her dress?

"Allow me to escort you downstairs," she said, determined to prove that she could act the part of his wife. "Sam, please go in front of your master and myself, so that I shall know which way the dining-room lies."

Sam, nonplussed at this sudden show of authority from his former prisoner, did not move from Lord Danewood's side. He started to speak, looked at Janet, and fell silent.

"Sam," said Lord Danewood gently. "Please do as your mistress asks."

"Yes, m'lord." The servant moved with evident reluctance towards the door, holding it open for his master and mistress to pass through. Lord Danewood rested his hand lightly on the surface of Elizabeth's arm and bent his head to whisper in her ear.

"Don't think of tripping me, my dear, because Sam would undoubtedly catch me. A wasted act of petty revenge, and you would find yourself deprived of a good chance to earn a thousand pounds."

Elizabeth replied through tight lips. "I have said that I will help you, my lord, and I have no

107

intention of going back on my word. I have given *you* no cause to doubt *my* integrity."

"Now what the devil do you mean by that remark?" he asked.

"That is hardly proper language to use with your wife, my lord," Elizabeth said forgetting in the heat of the moment that she was not actually his wife. She gave a tiny gasp of horror when she realized the treacherous direction of her own thoughts. Less than four hours in Danewood Hall, and already she was believing her own lies! It was a relief to see that Sam had come to a halt.

"This is the dining-room, your ladyship," he said.

In the ordinary course of events, Elizabeth would have felt overwhelmed by the intimidating size of the dining-hall. An ancient chamber that had survived from the original building, it was heavily draped in thick red brocade and furnished with a new oaken dining table of surpassing size and ugliness. She certainly ought to have felt some nervousness at meeting David Vincent, the cousin and heir who loved Lord Danewood's former betrothed.

Fortunately for her, she was too annoyed with herself and Lord Danewood to have much room left for experiencing other emotions. She greeted Mr. Vincent with an absent-minded regality which had all the servants nodding their heads in secret approval. Since The Master had gone completely mad and married a woman nobody had ever heard of, it was gratifying to see that he had at least retained sufficient sense to marry a lady.

David Vincent seemed not at all put out by Elizabeth's curt words of greeting. He smiled at her with a warmth that lit up his whole face and waited in courteous silence until a footman had assisted her into the chair at the foot of the monstrous table. Lord Danewood, with Sam once more at his side, spoke quietly to the butler.

"Are the places for Mr. Vincent and myself laid on either side of Lady Danewood? I don't plan to shout myself hoarse trying to conduct a conversation down the length of this table."

David Vincent gave a rueful laugh. "It certainly is a monstrosity. I imagine that changing the decorative scheme of this room will be one of your first tasks, Lady Danewood. I'm afraid that I feel a personal responsibility for its gloomy appearance. After the death of the late Lady Danewood, Roderick's mother, my own mother took over the task of running this house. This room, I regret to confess, is the result of her efforts to modernize the ancient dining-chamber."

Elizabeth managed at last to bring her distracted attention back to David Vincent, and she looked up to give him her friendliest smile. He was so handsome, she thought, that it was no wonder the beautiful Clarissa Fanshawe had lost her heart.

"The decoration is not the style I would choose for myself," she said. "But I don't think we can hold ourselves responsible for the tastes of our parents, do you? That is too great a burden for a young person to carry. Our own indiscretions are wearisome enough!"

"Do you think so?" said David Vincent, responding to the friendliness of Elizabeth's manner. "Your own taste, if I may be permitted to say so, seems exquisite." He turned to Lord Danewood who had remained silent. "Your wife's gown, Roderick, is the creation of a genius."

"I'm glad you approve," said Lord Danewood. He took a sip of wine before turning towards Elizabeth. "David is noted for his fashion-sense, my dear, so you are entitled to feel flattered."

Elizabeth detected the faintest undercurrent of contempt in Lord Danewood's flat tones. She glanced hurriedly at David Vincent to see if he appeared offended. She was relieved to find him smiling at her, his expression giving no hint of resentment towards Lord Danewood. She was struck anew by the handsome appearance of his features. His eyes were a deep, soft brown, and she found herself gazing at them, wondering once again what colour Lord Danewood's eyes might be. Strange to think that she didn't yet know such a simple detail as the colour of her supposed husband's eyes. Perhaps she could ask him some day, if they were ever alone together, away from the ubiquitous Sam.

"I'm pleased that my wife meets your fastidious standards, David." Lord Danewood had his dark glasses fixed in Elizabeth's direction, and his voice broke with unexpected harshness into her reverie. "For myself, I confess that I was bowled over at our first meeting."

"And where was that, Lady Danewood?" David twisted back to smile at Elizabeth.

"We...we met in London," she said and took a hasty gulp from her wineglass. The information seemed hopelessly scanty, so she added lamely, "We met at a dinner party, you know."

David did not seem to be paying much attention to her flustered explanations, since he was studying her profile with frank admiration. "I can quite understand how, as soon as Roderick saw you, he had a special place for you in his heart."

There was an immediate and uncomfortable silence around the table, David Vincent looked stricken. "So sorry, Roddy old chap," he mumbled at last. "I keep forgetting."

"Don't apologize," said Lord Danewood after a short pause. "I am flattered that you find my deficiencies so easy to overlook. I, on the other hand, am very much aware of all that I'm missing in not seeing Elizabeth's lovely face. It was her voice that first attracted me to her."

David gestured to one of the footmen and indicated that his plate should be taken away. He had eaten little, she saw, and her own appetite seemed to have vanished. She watched while David fiddled unhappily with the stem of his wineglass.

"What did the doctors say this time, Roderick?" he asked finally.

Lord Danewood lifted his shoulders in a delicate shrug. "What do they always say? A different opinion from each specialist, all of them offering optimism if only I am prepared to wait patiently for the next twenty years."

"They don't think the condition is permanent, then?" David asked quickly. "That, surely, is a new note of hope."

Lord Danewood did not disguise the cynicism of his reply. "They probably wish to make sure that I pay them another visit in May. Who knows what they will tell me on the next trip?"

Elizabeth stretched out her hand in an impulsive gesture of encouragement. "Oh no! I don't think so, Roderick. If there were irreversible damage, any reputable doctor would know that by now."

For the shortest moment, Elizabeth thought she saw Lord Danewood's harsh features soften into tenderness, but almost immediately he turned away from her with one of his familiar, derisive smiles. "How good it is to hear the reassurances of a loving wife!" Abruptly he spoke to his cousin. "Will you take care of Elizabeth for me tomorrow, David? Show her something of Danewood and the estate. I have been called to an...urgent... appointment with Mr. Fanshawe."

A young footman dropped the serving dish he was carrying, scattering boiled potatoes all over the dining-room floor. Lord Danewood continued eating roast beef without so much as turning his head in the direction of the noise. Elizabeth and David Vincent, finding it more difficult to feign deafness, squirmed uneasily in their chairs.

"I shall be delighted to escort Lady Danewood." David's polite words succeeded in covering up the mumbles of confusion coming from the footman.

Lord Danewood appeared oblivious to the mounting tension in the dining-room. "Elizabeth knows all about my betrothal to Clarissa, you know. There's absolutely no need for you to be so discreet."

David flushed and his embarrassed gaze flickered helplessly between Elizabeth and the butler, who was directing two young housemaids in their search for boiled potatoes. She forced herself to smile at David, silently furious with Lord Danewood for his lack of tact. Because she felt so uncomfortable at Lord Danewood's maladroit behav-

112

iour, she had no difficulty in presenting a picture of rosy-cheeked confusion to David Vincent.

"Everything was so sudden," she whispered in apparent explanation. "Roderick promised me that Miss Fanshawe wanted to be released from her betrothal."

David cast an anguished glance of warning in the direction of the servants. He clearly didn't share Lord Danewood's sublime indifference to the crowd of domestic observers. "Do you ride, Lady Danewood? If the weather continues fine tomorrow, it would be delightful to see some of the estate on horseback."

"I ride indifferently, Mr. Vincent. I have not had much opportunity to improve my skills."

"She lived in Liverpool, you know," interjected Lord Danewood cheerfully. "It's a busy city and not clean enough for the ladies to ride around without the protection of a well-upholstered carriage."

"Oh yes, of course." David Vincent was obviously no happier discussing Elizabeth's supposed origins in Liverpool than he was in discussing the absent Miss Fanshawe. "Well, if it's fine we can drive in my curricle. I have recently taken delivery of a new one, and I'll be happy to show you just how well modern carriages can be sprung."

"David doesn't share your enthusiasm for the railways, my dear," said Lord Danewood. Elizabeth stared angrily at the dark screen of his tinted glasses. As always, it was impossible for her to guess what he was thinking, although his voice conjured up images of a sleek, well-fed cat, poised outside a mousehole. David was such a personable young man that she couldn't understand why his manner reminded her irresistibly of the frightened mouse pursued by Lord Danewood's cat.

Once again, however, David's reply gave no hint of animosity towards his cousin. "It would be a dull world if we all enjoyed the same things, Roderick. We can't all share your addiciton to mechanical inventions." He smiled lightly at his cousin. Elizabeth began to wonder if she had become so used to sensing unspoken resentment around her father's dinner table that she now suspected hidden tensions where none actually existed. She searched David's face when he turned towards her, and saw nothing save courtesy and friendliness reflected in his gentle eyes. "If you are not too fatigued by your journey, Lady Danewood, then I shall look forward to escorting you tomorrow morning. Shall we say ten o'clock?"

"That would be most agreeable," she said. She gave up her pretence of eating dessert. Quite apart from the fact that her stomach churned with nervous tension, several weeks of captivity had still not accustomed her to the enormous meals people kept serving her. She seized the opportunity presented by David Vincent's words and half rose from her chair. The butler and a footman sprang to her assistance. Perhaps because her composure was threatened by fatigue, she had to fight against the urge to giggle. Having been taught from early childhood that the wage of sin was eternal damnation, she seemed to be proving that her reward for disobedience was a life led in the lap of luxury. She conquered the impulse to laugh by the simple device of imagining what her father—or Mr.

Hodge—would have to say if they could only observe her.

She inclined her head in a gesture of thanks towards the servants, who still supported her delicately beneath the elbows. "With your kind permission, Mr. Vincent, I think I shall retire. The journey from London has fatigued me more than I at first suspected."

David murmured a polite acknowledgement and Lord Danewood, unobtrusively assisted by Sam, rose from his seat. He reached out for Elizabeth's hands and somewhat reluctantly she placed her fingers within his clasp. He raised her hand to his lips and slowly, with deliberate emphasis, kissed the tip of each finger.

"I shall not keep you waiting long, my dear." He spoke softly, but she was quite sure that his cousin could hear what was said. "I shall come and bid you goodnight upstairs."

She was flustered by his manner, which was quite unlike his usual cool reserve. She felt herself blush and turned quickly back towards David. "Until tomorrow morning than, Mr. Vincent."

He bowed low over her hand. "I am looking forward to furthering our relationship, Lady Danewood."

She found that her legs were trembling when she closed the dining-room door behind her. She couldn't account rationally for this excess of emotion and attributed her condition to the stresses of a long journey. When she got back to her room, she was pleased to find Janet waiting for her.

It was soothing to stand by the fire in her bedroom and allow the maid to fuss with tiny pearl buttons, endless rows of hooks and long strings of white ribbons. It was a pleasure to slip into the soft smoothness of her new bedgowns, made of the sheerest linen. It was terrible to think that all this had been paid for by Lord Danewood, of course, but that didn't alter the fact that sheer linen was wonderfully comfortable to sleep in.

She experienced a shock of pleasure when she slid between the sheets of the bed and felt warmth radiating out from the stone hot-water bottles placed beneath the covers. She was delighted to find this luxurious practice continued here at Danewood Hall. She had been afraid it might be a luxury confined to the decadence of the city. She leaned back against the plump pillows of the bed. Her sensation of physical well-being successfully masked the lingering strains of the evening.

Of course Lord Danewood wouldn't really come into her bedroom. The thought sprang into her mind and was pushed swiftly away. His fond parting at the dinner-table had been enacted for the benefit of David Vincent and for the servants.

"Shall I extinguish the candles, my lady?" Janet's prosaic question put an end to useless speculation.

"Yes, please." The house in London had been lit entirely by modern gas-lamps. They had been wonderfully efficient but Elizabeth hadn't become accustomed to the constant, frightening hiss of burning gas. She was glad Danewood Hall still retained old-fashioned wall-sconces. "Good night, Janet. Thank you for your help today."

"Good night, my lady," Janet picked up her candlestick and curtsied when she reached the door to the sitting-room.

"What time would your ladyship wish me to bring your breakfast?"

"At eight o'clock perhaps?" In Barclay Manor she had always been up with the dawn. But in Barclay Manor she had usually been in bed by nine o'clock at night. It seemed as though that Elizabeth Barclay was already a person without substance, a girl whose quiet existence had no connection with this new Elizabeth, the supposed Lady Danewood.

She nestled down into the soft, clean bed with a sigh. If she hadn't felt so sleepy she would have tried to decide upon some clever way of getting a message to her mother to let her know she was safe and well. But tonight her eyelids were too heavy and sleep began to steal over her.

She flung a protesting hand over her eyes when the light from an oil lamp cast its intrusive beam over her face. For a moment she was not sure whether she was awake or asleep when she heard the murmur of Lord Danewood's voice in her sitting-room.

"Thank you, Sam. You may safely leave me now."

The light was immediately withdrawn and Elizabeth shot up in bed as she heard the click of a closing door. All lingering traces of sleep vanished as she became aware of the dim shape of Lord Danewood, sitting on the edge of her bed.

"You are not very welcoming, my dear," he said. "I didn't expect to find you tucked away under the covers."

"And I certainly didn't expect you to come to my room, my lord. After all, we are only pretending to be married." She wriggled deeper under the bedcovers as she spoke. She was embarrassed to be receiving Lord Danewood in her bedroom after she had retired for the night. Surely, she thought, such an action must represent the ultimate peak of forbidden behaviour. She did her best not to think about Mama. "I wouldn't have dismissed the maid, my lord, if I had realised that you meant to bid me a second goodnight."

He did not reply at once and she snatched the sheet so that she could pull it more firmly under her chin, despite the fact that it was very dark in the bedroom. She felt foolish when she remembered that Lord Danewood could not see her, however much light there was in the room. Perhaps he felt that his blindness entitled him to break the strict rules concerning the behaviour of a gentleman towards a lady.

Despite her sympathy for his handicap, Elizabeth found his presence disturbing and her cheeks burned with flaming colour as his gaze turned upon her face. Although she knew he couldn't see, she was flooded with shame as his eyes, unfettered tonight by protective spectacles or concealing bandages, rested upon her.

"Did you have something especially urgent to say to me, my lord?" For some reason, she found it easier to speak than to remain silent.

"I hardly think words are necessary, my dear, do you? Delightful as your conversation sometimes proves, I don't think this is the moment for indulging in an exchange of witticisms."

Elizabeth's eyes were becoming accustomed to the darkness of the bedroom. "Your eyes!" she exclaimed, ignoring his remarks. "They don't seem to be scarred at all! I'm so glad."

She forgot all about the impropriety of his presence in her bedroom in the excitement of the moment. She leaned forward and rested her hand against his cheek, feeling the faint ridge of a faded scar. "What colour are your eyes, my lord? I was wondering about that only this evening, thinking how little we truly know about one another."

Lord Danewood jerked his head sharply away from her touch and passed his hand quickly across his eyes, shielding them from her gaze. "I prefer not to discuss the subject of my sight," he said quickly. "My eyes were...are...some indeterminate shade between brown and grey."

"I understand why you don't wish to talk about your accident," she said softly. "But you mustn't give up hope, my lord. If the surface of your eyes wasn't burned, nature will surely effect a cure at some time in the future—perhaps even more swiftly than you now think possible."

He jumped up from the bed and turned away from her. "I have asked you to leave the subject of my accident quite alone." He walked quickly across her bedroom, managing to avoid knocking into any of the chairs and side-tables scattered across the floor. For Lord Danewood, she realized, the darkness of her room presented no new obstacle. Her heart softened as she imagined what he must feel, locked into permanent darkness.

"Thank you for coming in to say good-night," she said. The sympathy she felt for his plight mellowed her voice into tenderness. "Shall I ring the bell to summon Sam, so that he can escort you back to your own bedroom?"

He laughed. "Good God, Elizabeth, there's no need to pretend when we are alone. I have no intention of leaving just yet. I was busy while we were in London, but for a thousand pounds, my dear, I expect more from you than tender professions of concern about my eyes. You have done a good job of playing the loving wife for the benefit of Cousin David. You have convinced the servants here at Danewood that I wasn't mad to have married you. Now let's see if I am to derive any personal pleasure from this masquerade."

He came back to the bed and ran his hands lightly over her face. "Such perfectly regular features," he murmured. His hands moved to gather up a cluster of chestnut hair. "To think that all this is achieved without curling irons! It seems hardly fair to the other members of your sex." He stretched his body on to the bed and pulled Elizabeth's face close to his own. "I'm sure you have kissable lips," he said softly. "I'm amazed that I have waited so long to find out." His lips pressed a teasing kiss on the dimple in her cheek, before moving with sudden aggression to cover her entire mouth. Paralysed with horror, and yet aware of the faint stirrings of some other emotion, she felt the pressure of Lord Danewood's lips against her teeth, even as his hands undid the ribbons of her nightgown.

Shaking with a flood of emotion it was impossible to identify, she tore herself from his arms. She sprang out of the bed and seized a blanket to drape around her body, stark terror blocking her powers of speech.

"Are you run mad?" she croaked at last. "What...what were you trying to do with me? We aren't really married, so you cannot...we can't..." Her voice deserted her, overwhelmed by the impossibility of describing what had just occurred on the bed.

He rose to his feet and pulled her to him with unconcealed menace. "I don't know what game you think you're playing, Elizabeth, but I don't find it amusing. I already told you at Madam Portunio's that I have no interest in deflowering virgins. Pray spare us both a disagreeable and boring performance of shocked innocence. It really isn't necessary, you know."

She couldn't disguise the shudders that racked her body when Lord Danewood again pulled her into his arms. She tried to speak calmly.

"Please, my lord, let me go. I don't understand what you're saying, but I know that what you want to do is wrong."

He stopped his kisses and put his hand tightly against Elizabeth's breast. Beneath his fingers, her heart raced at frightening speed, and he could hear her breath emerge from her throat in tiny gasps as though each intake of air was an effort. With his other hand he reached down to touch her fingers. They were icy cold to his touch. As roughly as he had pulled her to him, he pushed her away again.

"If I didn't know such a thing was impossible, I would have said you are genuinely terrified. Even if by some unlikely chance you're still a virgin, why do you find it so impossible to submit to me? You have presumably been trained for your profession and you were willing to sell yourself to the highest bidder among Madam Portunio's other clients. Although I'm blind, which you may find repelling, she had clients with worse afflictions."

Elizabeth's voice was flat with despair. There

seemed to be no way of convincing him that she didn't understand the accusations he hurled at her so frequently.

"Madam Portunio engaged me to serve tea and refreshments to her guests, nothing more. And in any case, I had only been there for one evening when you took me away." She dashed a hand across her eyes, which kept filling with tears despite her stubborn determination to hold them back. "I know I shouldn't have taken employment in a gambling establishment. I know Papa wouldn't have approved, but then he never approves of anything. However, Madam Portunio assured me that it was a *private* club and I also knew that I would find it very hard to secure a position as a governess, or even as a housekeeper. I have no references to offer, you see."

"You are either the world's best actress, or you are telling the truth," said Lord Danewood. "Were you so innocent that it escaped your notice that Madam Portunio was running a brothel? Good God, child, where did you spring from?" He broke off with an impatient exclamation. "Oh, damnation! Don't bother to answer that question. Tell me truthfully, once and for all, how did you end up at Madam Portunio's?"

She only needed to think for a minute before deciding that there was no point in concealing the truth any longer.

"I ran away from home," she said. "My father wanted me to marry Mr. H....I didn't want to get married to the man my father had chosen. I was looking for respectable lodgings and somebody directed me to Madam Portunio's house."

Lord Danewood's mouth twisted into a cynical

smile. "I don't doubt they did," he said. "Hell and damnation, I wish I didn't have to believe you! I'm afraid we've managed to make a terrible mess out of each other's affairs."

"I'm quite satisfied, my lord," she said eagerly, relieved that he was not pressing her with awkward questions about her home and her family. "Once your situation with Clarissa Fanshawe has been settled, I shall be delighted to leave for Europe. I ran away from home in order to start a new life. You are providing me with the means to make a fresh start possible."

Lord Danewood turned away with an impatient shrug of his shoulders. "I suppose that's one way of describing my actions. At least you were rescued from Madam Portunio's before that old harpy was able to do her worst." He put his hand up to his eyes with a sudden gesture of weariness. "Ring for Sam, Elizabeth, and I'll go back to my own room. There is no point in trying to think while I'm in your bedroom." He put out his hand and touched her lightly on the arm, but walked away from her as he felt a fresh tremor ripple through her.

"Will you be all right?" he asked curtly.

"Yes," she said, wondering why she felt a strange longing to rest her cheek against the smooth silk of Lord Danewood's dressing gown. "I shall be all right."

"You are trembling."

Elizabeth looked down at her hands, surprised to see that they still shook. "It's just that I'm cold," she said and wondered if it was true.

"Return to your bed, my dear. I promise you that you will be quite safe from any further unwelcome advances from me."

She climbed meekly beneath the covers, unable to give coherent form to the thoughts and feelings rushing through her mind in pell-mell confusion. She was pleased when she heard Sam's tap on the panels of the door and heard Lord Danewood's soft command to enter. He walked slowly across the bedroom and turned to speak to Elizabeth from the doorway of her private sitting-room.

"Good-night. We must talk again when I have seen Mr. Fanshawe and set matters right in that quarter."

"Yes, my lord." She scarcely absorbed the meaning of his words. Her thoughts were too incoherent to allow room for extraneous information.

The outer door closed with a quiet click and she fell back against the pillows, staring up at the white plaster mouldings of the ceiling. She could just discern the outline of a bunch of grapes in the silver moonlight filtering through a crack in the blinds.

It was impossible to make sense of the bewildering events of the past hour, but she had already taken one firm decision. Tomorrow she was going to discover the location of the Danewood library. Barclay Manor had not possessed a copy of Dr. Johnson's famous dictionary. But if Danewood Hall was better equipped, she was going to put an end to the mystery surrounding Madam Portunio and Lord Danewood. She was going to look up the meaning of the word *brothel*, then she might discover just why Lord Danewood so often seemed angry for no reason.

Carefully she stored the words in her mind. "Brothel," she murmured. "Virgin," she repeated, and fell asleep.

EIGHT

Mr. Vincent drove his curricle with considerable flair. His horses, a pair of lively bays, gave some initial signs of friskiness, but soon settled down under the skilful control of his hands upon the reins. Elizabeth noted approvingly that he resorted rarely to the whip and guided the animals with light pressure on the reins than by cruel cuts to their flanks.

They drove down the carriageway at a spanking pace and she felt some of the strain melt away from her. It was a perfect day, with the sun giving its first hint of real summer warmth, and she decided to put all troublesome thoughts out of her mind and surrender herself to the enjoyment of the moment.

She must have given an unconscious sigh of relaxation, for Mr. Vincent turned to her with a friendly smile. "I gather you've decided to trust my driving ability. Confess now, Lady Danewood, you suspected that I was about to run us into a ditch."

"No such thing!" she protested with an answering laugh.

"Then why the worried frowns?" he asked lightly. "If not my skill at the reins, what else could there be to trouble you on such a splendidly sunny morning?"

She turned to admire an ornamental lake, artfully framed by three drooping willows. She was glad of an excuse to hide her face. "You were imagining my frowns, Mr. Vincent, or at least I hope you were. I'm afraid I am always a bit grumpy in the morning."

"I don't believe that you could ever be grumpy, but I shall not press you for confidences," he said. "If I pause just at the crest of this small rise, you will have an excellent view of the front of the Hall. The facade is considered to be the supreme example of Palladian architectural styling in this region."

"I didn't know that," said Elizabeth, thinking how little she knew of her native country. Her father's stern regime had allowed no time for excursions to local points of interest.

"There is no reason why you should, is there? The fame of Danewood Hall cannot have reached as far as Liverpool and my cousin is not the sort of fellow to press his suit by boasting of the splendours of his family seat."

"No, indeed he is not." Anxious to turn the conversation before she gave away the fact that she had lived all her life in Berkshire, Elizabeth spoke admiringly of the use of marble and the elegance of the Queen Anne porticos which adorned the Hall. David Vincent responded to all her remarks with such candid enthusiasm and modest family pride that her opinion of the young man rose constantly.

They drove round the park for almost two hours, their conversation roaming widely. She watched his flush of pride as he described some land reclamation planned by his grandfather and she smiled at him with unaffected friendliness. She found herself wishing that he might really have been her cousin.

"We are relatives now, Mr. Vincent, and formality between us is unnecessary. My name if Elizabeth and I wish that you would use it."

"And I hardly need to say how pleased I should be if you would call me David." They smiled, in harmony with the day and with each other.

In their new mood of intimacy, she found the deception she was practising upon him more irksome than before. She chafed under the need to lie to him about her marriage to Lord Danewood. Even as she hesitated upon the brink of a partial confession, her attention was caught by a blackened cluster of buildings, huddled at the edge of three or four acres of fenced pasture.

"Oh! What's that?" she asked, although she already suspected the answer to her question.

"Those are the remains of the stables where Roderick kept his racing-horses, Elizabeth. Until the time of the accident he dabbled in horse-breeding. He was acquiring something of a reputation as the owner of several fine steeplechasers."

She looked at the blackened brick foundations walls and gave a small cry of protest when David turned his curricle sharply away from the pastures. "No, David! Let me see the stables. That's where my husband met with his accident, isn't it? Why hasn't he cleared the land and rebuilt the stables?"

David tooled his curricle down the narrow rutted path towards the paddocks. He was evidently reluctant to pander to Elizabeth's morbid wish to inspect the derelict buildings.

"Do you think a close examination of such an unhappy spot is wise, Cousin Elizabeth? Roderick himself cannot bear to come near the place and will have nothing more to do with his horses. The racing string has been sold and he no longer even speaks to the grooms and stablehands who care for the carriage animals."

"But Sam is always with him," said Elizabeth, pursuing her own train of thought and scarcely noticing that she spoke out loud. "And Sam was surely a groom before he became my husband's valet."

"Sam is a special case," said David shortly. "He discovered Roderick lying on the floor of the tack room and dragged him to safety. He exposed himself to considerable danger, wrapping himself in a farrier's leather apron and actually breaching a wall of flame to reach his master. It's no wonder that Roderick now reposes unique trust in Sam's loyalty and dedication." David gave a small, embarrassed laugh. "You must forgive me, Elizabeth, if I didn't seem very willing to bring you to this spot. I still find the memories of that...dreadful night, hard to endure."

His tormented words touched Elizabeth's heart. She couldn't close her mind to the vivid images of

Lord Danewood, spread-eagled on the ground, the hungry flames licking ever closer to his unconscious body. No wonder David preferred not to recall the events of that traumatic night!

She shuddered. It was hard to believe that this had once been the site of a busy racing stables. Almost nothing remained of the building except a few charred beams piled randomly against the smoke-stained bricks of the foundation. The paddocks, flat and devoid of trees, increased the barren atmosphere of the ruin. Another involuntary tremor shook her body and David Vincent looked up with immediate concern.

"You shouldn't have come, Elizabeth. It must be distressing for you to see the actual place of Roderick's accident. It's plain to me that you love him very much."

"Yes," she said. "I can't bear to think of such a powerful man permanently fettered by blindness." She faltered into silence as the significance of her own words penetrated her consciousness. She blushed a deep scarlet and turned her face hastily away from the unwelcome discernment of David's gaze. Fortunately he didn't press any further questions upon her.

"I will drive you into the village," he said. "It's only small, but Roderick and his father have been benign landlords and the cottages are in such a good state of repair that the overall effect is most pleasing. The cottagers take great pride in their gardens and always plant a few bright flowers among the cabbages and potatoes."

She replied with some comment upon the beauty of spring flowers and the moment of intimacy passed. They toured the picturesque village and

Elizabeth was careful to keep their talk upon trivial matters until David turned his curricle on to the long gravel driveway which led up to the front of Danewood Hall. Elizabeth could hardly believe that it was less than twenty-four hours since she had obtained her first glimpse of that imposing facade.

She spoke abruptly to David, interrupting his commentary upon the problems of landscaping flat gardens without even realizing that she had done so. "Was he very ill after the accident?" she asked.

"Hasn't my cousin told you anything about it?"

"No," she replied with perfect truth. "He doesn't want to talk about it."

"We feared for his life for several weeks and then, just when we hoped that all danger was past, his nurse made some error with the drugs prescribed by the doctor and he was almost poisoned by an overdose of sleeping-draught."

"He has never mentioned any of this to me," Elizabeth whispered. "He always seems so much in command. It's terrifying to think of him close to death on two separate occasions."

"The nurse was dismissed," said David reassuringly. "And Roderick now has you *and* Sam to ensure his well-being."

"And he may yet regain his sight," she said, more to comfort herself than to express a real possibility.

"Do you think so?" David asked quickly. "Have the surgeons given him more hope than he tells us?"

"I think not," she said, touched by David's evident concern for his cousin's health. "I'm afraid I was passing a personal judgment based upon nothing more substantial than the appearance of his eyes when he removes the bandages. Of course, I understand that there could well be permanent damage that is quite invisible."

"His eyes aren't scarred, however," David said. "He won't let anybody see him without the bandages or his dark glasses and so I had wondered."

"He has no visible scars," Elizabeth repeated. For some reason she was relieved to see that their curricle had drawn to a halt outside the entrance to the Hall. Their conversation, so carefully neutral after their tour of the ruined stables, had suddenly acquired a fresh note of intensity. She discovered that she was surprisingly reluctant to discuss the state of Lord Danewood's health with his cousin, probably because she revealed her own infatuation with every sentence she uttered.

"Thank you for a delightful morning," she said, giving him her most charming smile. "It would be hard to imagine a more attractive part of the country in which to live."

"An improvement over the smokestacks of Liverpool, I don't doubt." For a brief moment, Elizabeth thought she detected the hint of a sneer in David's voice, but when she looked up at him she saw nothing in his face save warmth and kindly feelings. She gave him another smile, feeling almost guilty at her ridiculous suspicions. Life with Papa in the confinement of Barclay Manor was certainly causing her to read double meanings into the most innocuous of statements.

"Will you be joining us for dinner again this evening, David? I do hope so."

"Oh, yes. I haven't yet had an opportunity to report to Roderick with an account of my stewardship." He gave a little laugh. "I shall not be released from duty until I have ridden round the estate and outlined the fate of every brick and every animal since Roderick's last tour."

"It must be a great relief to him to know that he has such a trustworthy pair of eyes to rely upon now that his own can no longer keep him informed." A groom and a young stable-lad had finally appeared from the yard at the side of the house and David sprang down from the curricle, offering his hand to Elizabeth.

"This will only be the first of many excursions, I trust," he said as he handed her down from the carriage. "Your presence will add a special attraction to my visits to Danewood."

"It will certainly be a delight to discover more about my new home with you as a guide." Her voice reflected the pleasure she had felt during the drive as she said goodbye. "Don't keep your horses standing, David. They are too fine to be permitted to take a chill."

"Until this evening, then." He bowed low over her hand, raising it to his lips in a gesture reminiscent of an earlier age. "It has been a wonderful morning for me."

Lord Danewood's visit to the Honourable Henry Fanshawe at Oak House had evidently not gone well. One of the grooms was sent back from Oak House with a message saying that Lord Danewood was detained and would not be dining at home. Elizabeth was quite glad to learn that she could take a peaceful meal alone with David Vincent. She was in no hurry to cross swords with Lord

Danewood again, particularly when she was feeling so sleepy.

She had hoped to spend the afternoon in the library—she hadn't forgotten her resolution to find a copy of Dr. Johnson's famous dictionary—but the housekeeper had other plans. Mrs. Pritchard, a formidable woman whose overflowing curves were tightly encased in a tucked-and-gathered bodice of black bombazine, insisted upon escorting Elizabeth through every storeroom and cupboard in Danewood Hall. Peering into shelves of white linen, smelling faintly of dried lavender, and glancing over stillroom shelves packed with glass jars of pickles and preserves, Elizabeth could only profess herself overwhelmed by the evidence of Mrs. Pritchard's industry. The housekeeper didn't give up her ruthless tour of immaculate rooms and stores of polished furniture until the afternoon light was already fading into dusk.

She returned from this housekeeping tour to find Janet anxiously pacing her sitting-room, muttering that there was scarcely sufficient time for her ladyship to change into the simplest of outfits suitable for dinner. The maid seemed almost relieved to learn that Lord Danewood would not be dining at home, and relaxed slightly as she twitched her mistress's grey silk gown in place over the hoops of her new crinoline. Elizabeth was diverted by this unconscious revelation of domestic snobbery. Lord Danewood, who couldn't see, required a perfectly-outfitted wife. David Vincent, who could appreciate her toilette, only merited her second-best silk dinner dress and no special hairstyle.

The day had been tiring however, and there was

no denying the fact that dinner with David Vincent was less of an ordeal (and less exciting) than dinner with Lord Danewood. There was no subterfuge in her sleepy apology to David as soon as dinner was over. She could scarcely swallow the yawns that threatened to overcome her.

"David, I do apologise," she said as she felt herself drooping over the tea-tray. "You'll have to forgive me. I'm not accustomed to such late nights."

David covered his startled expression with a quick smile. "It's only just past nine o'clock, Elizabeth!"

"Then it must be the fresh country air after so many days of London smoke. Whatever the cause, David, you will have to let me retire, or I'll be falling asleep on the sofa."

"Let me ring for your maid." David was immediately all concern. "You are evidently not yet recovered from the travelling. One can see how fragile your constitution must be."

Elizabeth was jerked out of her state of somnolence. "Heavens, David, you mistake the matter, I can assure you. I believe I have the most robust of constitutions, and can never manage to produce any of those useful symptoms of feminine delicacy. I don't believe I have ever fainted and I can scarcely remember the last time I had a headache."

She could have kicked herself as soon she had spoken. Why on earth had she insisted on the perfect state of her health, when Lord Danewood was shortly planning to claim that she had expired of a wasting fever? It was proving extraordinarily difficult to remember all the details of their plot.

She got up swiftly, before she could make any further mistakes. "Goodnight, David. Perhaps I may rely upon you tomorrow to give me a conducted tour of the village church? The housekeeper tells me it's a fine example of late Norman architecture."

"It will be my pleasure, Elizabeth." David rose to his feet. "I'm only sorry that our evening together has been so short."

Her slumber was so deep and immediate after Janet had left her for the night that Elizabeth was unable to understand why she woke up. At one moment she was lost to the world and at the next she was wide awake, lying comfortably in bed, but alert to every creak and groan in the floorboards.

She lay listening to the small sounds that broke the night-time silence. She had no candle and it was too dark to see the time on the elegant ormulu clock which graced her mantelpiece, but she felt sure it was very late. Some impulse drew her to the window and, pushing back the thick velvet curtains, she was able to see that the first pale fingers of dawn were poking grey light into the blackness of the sky. She wrapped herself into the pink robe the maid had left lying on the chaiselongue, nestling her shoulders into the fluffy swansdown trimming, rubbing her cheeks softly against the floating, airy strands of fur. With the curtains drawn partly back, faint light fell on her dressing-table mirror, illuminating her reflection with an ethereal, ghostly glow.

Elizabeth touched her heavy brown curls, pushing them back from her shoulders with a self-conscious gesture, before turning impatiently from the shadowy reflection. She slipped her feet into the soft pink slippers placed by the side of her bed, and tried not to think about the pleasure she derived from the frivolity and useless luxury of her new clothes.

She had to search for some time to find a tinder to light her candle. The servants obviously felt she should leave such menial tasks to them. Having succeeded in finding a light, she crept out of her room into the huge upstairs hallway. It was chilly away from the low-burning fires of her bedroom, and she hurried down the stairs. She didn't conceal herself intentionally, but from force of habits acquired in Barclay Manor she moved quietly staying close to the wall. In the downstairs hall she hesitated, still confused by the haphazard layout of the innumerable rooms. She opened the one door only to discover that it led to a small breakfast parlour, and a second door gave on to some sort of office. On the third guess, however, she discovered the library and with a sigh of relief she walked into the room.

So great was her satisfaction in discovering the library, that she didn't pause to light all the candles. She touched a spill to one of the oil lamps and placed it on the mantelpiece, using her own candle to examine the contents of the library shelves.

The books were carefully ordered, she soon found out. A collection of Latin texts was grouped on one shelf, followed by a selection of Greek poetry. She almost forgot her real purpose in coming to the library when she came upon a fascinating collection of modern novels. She spent several enraptured moments dipping into the pages of Sir Walter Scott before returning the book to its resting place. She stood back and scanned the shelves as far as her eyes could reach, hoping fervently that the dictionaries and lexicons were not going to be tucked away close to the ceiling. She had convinced herself that she would never understand Lord Danewood's strange flashes of rage until she had looked up the meaning of the words he hurled at her in tones of such bitter accusation.

She walked soundlessly to a fresh section of shelving and discovered a small selection of books devoted to English grammar. There was, however, no dictionary. Disconcerted, she pushed the grammar-books to one side, reaching behind them on the shelf to see if a dictionary had slipped behind the lesson-books.

"What the devil do you think you're doing?"

Elizabeth heard the movement from the doorway and whirled round, clutching the dictionary she had just discovered close to her body. She blushed a fiery red, aware that she looked the picture of guilt but unable to control her reactions. She plucked at the parting folds of her pink swansdown robe.

"I...I didn't know there was anybody here," she said.

"That is patently obvious," said Lord Danewood. "I've been following you on your mysterious wanderings ever since you left your bedroom. Just what did you hope to discover in my library of all places?"

"I came downstairs for a book," she said. "I woke up," she added as if that explained everything.

Lord Danewood smiled satirically. "A most persuasive story," he said. "May I be permitted to see your choice? It caused you such difficulty to remove it from the shelf. I'm curious to see what inspired you to scrabble around at the back of a pile of books when the room is filled with volumes that could have been yours for the mere stretching out of a hand."

With great reluctance she handed over the dictionary.

Lord Danewood glanced at the binding and laughed. "Come, come, my dear! Surely you could have grabbed something slightly more convincing even though I startled you."

She blushed again, angry with herself and annoyed that she needed to reveal her ignorance.

"I wanted to look up the meaning of a word. I'm tired of listening to accusations that I don't understand."

He frowned. "What word?"

"Brothel," she said fiercely, throwing caution to the winds. "I wanted to find out once and for all what sort of establishment Madam Portunio was running."

His frown deepened. He flicked over the pages of the book and handed it back to Elizabeth. "Here," he said brusquely. "You may read the entry for yourself."

Elizabeth took the dictionary and glanced down at the page he had indicated. She didn't bother to read very far before she looked up, her face whiter than the pages in front of her.

"You read the title of the book," she said flatly. "You turned to the correct page. You can *see*!"

"So I can," said Lord Danewood. "Life is full of little surprises, is it not?"

She ignored the sarcasm of his reply. "But that's wonderful! When did your sight return?"

"Just after somebody persuaded my night-nurse to poison me."

"You are referring to the accident with the sleeping-draught? But I understood...that is to say, your cousin David told me that that incident occurred months ago!"

Lord Danewood walked to the fireplace. He lit a taper from the oil-lamp and poked it into the piles of wood and paper laid in the fireplace. When the flames started to curl round the pieces of wood, he answered Elizabeth's question.

"I was only blind for six weeks after my accident," he said finally. "I have been able to see since last December. The surgeon and the physician whom I saw in London last month both agree that there has been no lasting damage to my eyes. They described my loss of sight as 'hysterical blindness' caused by the blow to the head and the shock of being trapped by fire." His lips twisted into a bitter smile. "If you have watched a stable full of maddened horses burn to death, Elizabeth, you will understand why a man's mind might prefer temporary blindness."

She sank down into the chair by the fire. "But what you are saying makes no sense. If you could see, why did you pretend that you could not?"

Lord Danewood looked at her, his expression hardening even as his eyes drank in the tumble of chestnut curls and the softness of her parted lips. "Why am I telling you all this?" he murmured harshly. "*That* is a case of madness if ever there was one."

"How can you say such a thing?" Elizabeth rose hurriedly from the chair and knelt down beside him, resting her hand on his knee. "If you can't confide in me, in whom should you confide? After all, I am your *wife*."

She looked earnestly into his eyes and saw the tension there relax into his familiar derisive smile. Immediately she realised what she had just said and corrected herself somewhat feebly. "Well...that is to say, I'm pretending to be your wife and you know that you can trust my discretion."

"Do I?" It seemed to be almost against his will that Lord Danewood stretched out his hand and allowed it to rest for a moment among the curls covering Elizabeth's shoulders. "All I know is that you're very beautiful and that you have been driving me to distraction ever since I first saw you in the clear light of day. You were trying to describe to me the beauty of the daffodils in my garden, and I could think only of the beauty within my bookroom."

Elizabeth tried to ignore the fact that his hands now caressed her shoulders in a fashion which was giving rise to a series of most extraordinary sensations. "But why, my lord?" she asked. "Why, in heaven's name, are you deceiving your family and friends as to the state of your health?" A fresh thought struck her and she gazed at him in horror. "I have just remembered Clarissa Fanshawe! Why this elaborate masquerade to free yourself from Miss Fanshawe when there is no reason why the marriage shouldn't go ahead?"

"There is an excellent reason," said Lord Danewood tranquilly. "I no longer wish to marry Clarissa."

"That's all very well," said Elizabeth. "But there's no need to pretend to be married to me in order to avoid marriage to Clarissa Fanshawe." She thrust her hands into her hair in a gesture of bewilderment. "I must have been temporarily deranged when I listened to you in London! How *could* I have accepted such a feeble excuse as an explanation for all this planning and scheming!"

He got up abruptly from his chair and paced restlessly around the room. "It's true that Clarissa doesn't want to marry me. It's also true that Mr. Fanshawe wouldn't permit her to break the engagement."

"I think I'm entitled to know why you brought me to Danewood Hall. We are both agreed that it has nothing to do with Clarissa Fanshawe."

She kept her gaze fixed on the leaping flames of the fire. It was less disturbing than watching Lord Danewood's powerful strides as he crossed and re-crossed the floor of the library.

"I am a very wealthy man," he said inconsequentially before lapsing once more into silence. "When my sight first returned, it came gradually," he said at last. "One day I was aware of light penetrating where before there had been only darkness. The next day, I felt sure I could see vague shapes moving about my room. I said nothing to my doctor or to my visitors because I wanted to be sure of the improvement before raising people's hopes. I was still pretty much confined to my bed with a couple of cracked ribs that had not completely healed. Falling timber, or something else, had knocked me about quite a bit long before the flames and smoke started to engulf me."

Elizabeth came and stood close to Lord Danewood, halting his restless pacing. She hated to see how the memories of pain tautened his mouth and etched the familiar lines of tension along his cheeks. Gently she touched her fingers to his lips. "It's over now, my lord," she said softly.

His eyes darkened with emotion as he gazed down into her face. She wondered how she could have believed, even in the darkness of her bedroom, that these passionate eyes had been sightless when they had looked at her the previous night. For a moment she thought Lord Danewood was going to kiss her and she shook with pleasurable anticipation, but as suddenly as he had drawn her close to him, he pushed her away. "Ah, no!" he murmured. "Not that! It would be too easy to turn my own weapons against me."

She flushed with mortification, not understanding the significance of his words, but well aware that she had thrown herself into his arms with an abandonment that no gentleman could expect to experience from a lady. She clutched the folds of pink swansdown closer to her neck and said with an attempt at coolness, "What happened next? You were telling me about the days when you found your sight returning."

"I couldn't see properly, and I was suffering from severe headaches, but on the very night that I first became capable of distinguishing shapes and movements, I became aware of somebody moving stealthily around my bedroom. There was always a glass of lemon juice left by my bedside and as soon as I had drunk it, I was aware of the violent pains and hallucinations. The person in my bedroom, whether it was the nurse or someone else I have no way of knowing, waited to observe my contortions and then went out of the room."

"Oh, no, my lord!" She rejected the accusations

with a gesture of revulsion. "You say yourself that the liquid caused you to hallucinate. How can you be sure that this silent figure is not a figment of your dreams? How can you claim that the person moved stealthily when you couldn't even see clearly enough to know whether or not the person was your nurse?"

"It was my sight which was impaired," said Lord Danewood curtly. "There was nothing wrong with my hearing."

Elizabeth didn't quite accept this explanation, but she was anxious to hear the end of the story. "Did somebody come in and find you, my lord?"

"No. I made my way into the dressing-room. Sam was sleeping there, as he had done every night since the fire."

The prosaic words created an uncomfortably vivid image of what Lord Danewood must have endured in removing himself from his bedroom to the dressing-room. "It was...it seemed a long walk, I expect," she said.

"I did not walk. I crawled," Lord Danewood said briefly.

She attempted to lighten the sudden tenseness of the atmosphere. "Well, at least you have survived to tell the tale," she said as cheerfully as she could.

"Oh yes," said Lord Danewood sardonically. "And I plan to discover who is trying to murder me as well."

She would have protested his words, urged him to consider how far his judgment could have erred under the pressures of a lengthy illness, but before she could say anything he seized her into his arms. He pulled her round, so that his back was facing

143

the door and thrust her full-length against his body. Then he bent his head and covered her mouth in a passionate kiss.

At first she was too shocked to feel anything at all, but gradually she felt her body softening against his and, with a small sigh, not even realising what she was doing, she put her hands up around his neck, holding his lips against her own.

Even as she swayed closer against him, she saw that the library door had been swung open and a cold draft of air rushed in from the hallway. Blushing furiously, embarrassed beyond speech at being discovered in Lord Danewood's arms, she tried to wriggle free. But Lord Danewood held her in an iron grip. His back, she realised, was still turned towards the door.

"Oh I say, I'm most frightfully sorry." David Vincent managed to sound almost as embarrassed as Elizabeth felt, his gaze shifting uncomfortably from her revealing pink wrap to Lord Danewood's back. "I heard a noise in here and wondered if we had burglars."

"Since we don't, old fellow, it might be more tactful if you withdrew. I don't believe Lady Danewood is dressed for receiving company."

"Oh...er...yes...Of course. Sorry again, and all that."

"Your apology is accepted. Or at least it would be if you would only get out."

The library door shut and they heard his footsteps beat a retreat down the marble-floored hall.

"He has gone." Lord Danewood sighed and released Elizabeth from his embrace. A small smile lit up the darkness of his eyes. "That was a very pleasant way of hiding my face. I should make sure in future that you're always on hand when I wish to keep my eyes hidden from somebody."

She was angry, chiefly because of her own ridiculous response to something Lord Danewood had considered nothing more than a piece of play-acting. "Why should you wish to hide your face, my lord? I can't see anything particularly repellent about it."

"Nobody—save you and Sam—has seen me without my dark glasses. I prefer to keep matters that way."

She was too angry with herself to pursue her questions any further. "It's nearly morning, my lord. I think it's time I returned to my own rooms, or I shall meet half the household between here and the upstairs hallway."

Lord Danewood walked back to the hearth and pulled a pair of dark spectacles out of his pocket, covering his eyes with the familiar black screen. "Don't forget the dictionary, my dear." He handed her the fat volume, which had lain neglected on the floor. "There are some words you wished to look up, I believe. I look forward to discussing the matter with you further when you discover exactly what sort of club Madam Portunio was running."

"That will no doubt be enjoyable for both of us," she said, accepting the book and trying to look dignified.

Lord Danewood's head inclined in an ironic salute. "We shall meet at dinner-time," he said. "If not before."

NINE

David Vincent was never able to take Elizabeth on the promised visit to St. Egburt's, the parish church. Lord Danewood threw himself into an orgy of work and David, together with the rest of the Danewood household, was fully occupied in keeping pace with his cousin's demands for information. Two dusty lawyers arrived from London and spent their days poring over the estate ledgers. At night the lawyers, together with David and Lord Danewood, held endless consultations in the library. David Vincent began to wear a grim expression of fatigue, mingled with worry. Lord Danewood seemed to thrive on this new regime of constant hard work.

Elizabeth didn't enquire about the reasons for this sudden activity, although Janet told her it was something to do with a new branch railway line. She was merely grateful for the rush of urgent business, whatever its cause. The lawyers, the piles of documents and the constant meetings, just made it that much easier for her to avoid any private encounter with Lord Danewood. She had checked the dictionary and discovered for herself the meaning of the words which had for so long bewildered her. In the light of her new and devastating information about Madam Portunio's so-called club, she could only hope that Lord Danewood would be kept busy until the very day it was time for his "wife" to travel abroad and "die."

In the meantime, since she was used to solitude, she had no trouble filling her days. She spent a great deal of time exploring the grounds, she performed the few household tasks Mrs. Pritchard allowed her to do, and thanked heaven every day that the neighbours were keeping away from Danewood Hall.

She was glad of this isolation. Her father had few personal friends, but in his position as squire of Barclay Manor he had developed a wide circle of acquaintance. She was uneasy at the thought that one of Lord Danewood's neighbours might have met her in the days when she had been Elizabeth of Barclay Manor.

Her relief at leading such a quiet life endured for nearly two weeks. The calm was shattered early one Sunday morning when Lord Danewood, escorted as always by Sam, appeared at the door of her sitting-room.

"I have come to remind you that we shall be attending Matins this morning, my love." Elizabeth's heart performed a somersault at the casual endearment, but Lord Danewood had already turned to chat with her maid. He finished a brief conversation with Janet and turned his dark gaze back towards Elizabeth. "In summer we occasionally delay our church-going until it's time for Evensong, but the drive is more pleasant in the morning. The early summer flowers in the hedgerows must be looking at their best."

She stared at him in dismay. "Perhaps we could talk privately, my l...Roderick." She allowed her glance to rest pointedly upon Sam and then upon Janet. She would never get used to Lord Danewood's easy informality in front of the servants.

He raised a quizzical eyebrow in her direction, causing her to blush uncomfortably. Nowadays she could guess the expression in his eyes as easily as if he hadn't been wearing thick, dark glasses. She couldn't understand why David Vincent and the servants remained unaware of the thread of silent mockery that ran through all his conversation with her.

"Sam, Janet," said Lord Danewood. "Perhaps you would leave us alone for a while." Without waiting to hear the door close, he turned to Elizabeth. "Sit down, my dear. If you're going to quarrel with me, you may as well do it in comfort."

"I prefer to stand," she said, struggling for composure. "You know very well that I can't accompany you to church."

He sat down in an overstuffed armchair, pulling off his spectacles, evidently at his ease. His eyes, she saw, were alight with laughter. "Why can't you go to church, my dear? Do you not possess a suitable bonnet?"

"I have a shelf full of suitable bonnets, as you know well," she replied. "You bought them for me yourself. But I can't go to church pretending to be your wife when we both know that you found me in a...in a...in the place that you did find me."

"Ah!" said Lord Danewood. "I perceive that you have been examining Dr. Johnson's admirable dictionary."

Colour flamed from Elizabeth's neck up into the roots of her hair. "I can't attend Morning Service when I'm pretending to be your wife," she said. "We both know that I'm a..." She swallowed hard. "I am a fallen woman, my lord."

He laughed. "Hardly that, my dear, although I should be most happy to offer you my services and help you to fall."

When she failed to reply, Lord Danewood rose from the chair and walked over to take her firmly in his arms, raising her chin so that she couldn't turn away from his inspection.

"I see that for you this isn't a matter that can be joked about," he said lightly. "My dear, you surely can't believe that the Almighty is about to let loose a thunderbolt in the Church because *you* have dared to attend Matins?"

"N-no," said Elizabeth, unable to conceal her uncertainty. "But it is so hypocritical, my lord."

He brushed the tips of her eyelashes with a gentle finger. "Tears, Elizabeth? Surely you are wise enough to know that you are being no more wicked in attending church than you are in consenting to stay here with me. And that, you know, is actually an act of kindness on your part. Besides, if our parish church allowed only those who are entirely virtuous within its walls, I can confidently predict that the Vicar would be preaching to rows of empty wooden pews!"

Elizabeth couldn't repress a smile. "I wonder

what your Vicar would say if he could hear you thus defaming his congregation?" She sighed, trying not very successfully to conceal her anxiety. "But there is also the question of your neighbours, my lord."

"A very dull lot," said Lord Danewood. "But I shall try to protect you from the worst of the bores."

"You know very well that I didn't mean to imply anything about their characters. It is *we* who are in error, my lord. It isn't right that I should be presented to them as Lady Danewood."

"Well, I can hardly present you to them as anything else," he said calmly. "What do you suggest? Should I say 'This is Elizabeth Barclay, whom I very much hope to make my mistress'?"

"You know full well that I want you to do no such thing. Are you never prepared to discuss anything seriously?"

"Not when we are so unlikely to come to an agreement." Lord Danewood put on his glasses, deliberately forming a barrier between them. "Elizabeth, soon I hope to speak to you at length, to tell you something more of what has been going on, but just for now I can't. You must trust me to see that no real harm comes from this masquerade. Come, put on that ravishing bonnet with the pink rosebuds and let's go to church. I'm looking forward to hearing you sing. I'm sure you have a delightful voice."

"I sing like a crow," she said mutinously just as Janet re-entered the room in response to Lord Danewood's tug at the bell-rope.

"I am going to have Sam escort me downstairs," he said to the maid. "I shall rely on you to finish dressing your mistress as quickly as possible. It wouldn't do if we were late on our first appearance together at church."

"Yes, my lord." Janet hurried into the bedroom to find Elizabeth's gloves, bonnet and wrap. Sam led Lord Danewood from the room, murmuring instructions so solicitously that Elizabeth would have sworn, if she hadn't known better, that Sam had no idea his master's eyesight was as good as his own.

David Vincent had travelled to church in his curricle and was already seated in the family pew when Elizabeth and Lord Danewood entered the thatched porch of St. Egburt's. The ripple of whispers rose and fell as they walked together down the aisle and seated themselves at the front of the church. She knew, however it might have seemed to the rest of the congregation, that it was Lord Danewood who supported her, his arm a steady rock beneath her quivering fingers. She resolved to concentrate her thoughts upon the stark beauty of the Norman church, despite the attention of a hundred pairs of eyes boring into her back.

The building dated from the early thirteenth century and the thick stone walls and narrow window slits were more reminiscent of a fortress than a place of worship. Nevertheless it seemed to Elizabeth that the greystone walls breathed out memories of centuries of prayer. The original windows were too narrow to give much light, but a magnificent modern stained-glass window behind the altar admitted a swirling kaleidoscope of jewelled sunlight.

The familiar words of Matins fell soothingly upon her ears. It was so dark inside the church that it would have been difficult to read the words of the service, but of course she knew every response by heart. It was not until the Vicar moved into the pulpit to deliver his sermon that she had any reason to look at him closely.

She gave an involuntary gasp as he started to preach and her knuckles gleamed white where she clutched her prayer book. David Vincent seemed unaware of her state of shock, but Lord Danewood turned to her at once.

"What is it?" he whispered.

"Nothing." She shook her head fiercely, determined to reject the evidence of her own eyes. Then, almost against her will, she allowed her gaze to travel up again to the face of the minister. In the dim light she couldn't discern every detail of his features, but she knew she hadn't been mistaken. She couldn't prevent the whispered question from tumbling out.

"What is the Vicar's name?" she asked.

"Mr. Adolphus Hodge," Lord Danewood answered. "He is a kind-hearted fellow who has been here for years. Why?"

She shook her head again. "We can't speak now." Her fingers relaxed their panic-stricken grip upon her Book of Common Prayer, although her stomach was still knotted with fright. Mr. *Adolphus* Hodge, so it wasn't the vicar from Barclay Manor. Perhaps this man was a cousin? She listened to the gentle words of his sermon, exhorting the congregation to greater kindness towards one another, urging tolerance for one another's small, unimportant weaknesses. Surely such a man could not be a close relative of Mr.

Clive Hodge, who saw sin lurking behind every smile and every gesture of happiness?

Her previous enjoyment of the service was at an end. She could think of nothing except the scandal that would break out if her deception was discovered. She closed her eyes, as if she could thus cut off the horrors her imagination was conjuring up. But it was no use. The same images pressed themselves into the darkness. Despairingly she looked back up at Mr. Hodge, quite expecting him to denounce her on the spot for the imposter that she was.

It was torture to remain seated for the rest of the service, standing up to sing the hymns as though nothing had occurred to remind her of the tightrope she was walking. Her misery finally became apparent to David Vincent who leaned across and touched her hand in a gesture of concern. "I say, Elizabeth, are you feeling quite the thing? You are frightfully pale, you know."

"I'm fine," she whispered. "Just a stupid sensation of faintness. Don't put any store by it, I beg."

There was no avoiding a round of introductions at the end of the service. Lord Danewood and his party left the church before any of the rest of the congregation stirred from the pews, but Elizabeth's hope of slipping away was a foolish one. It seemed to her that the lies about her supposed marriage had been repeated a hundred times before the Vicar walked across to join their little group. The only consolation was that the Fanshawes did not seem to be at church.

The Vicar smiled at her with unfeigned pleasure. "Welcome to Berkshire, Lady Danewood."

She held her breath, unable to continue with her pretence of composure, for surely no mere cousins had ever been as alike as Clive and Adolphus Hodge. Only the cheerful expression and the jovial mannerisms distinguished this man from the man who had once been chosen as her husband. His eyes, pale blue like those of Clive Hodge, twinkled up at Elizabeth with a jollity that had never appeared in Clive's eyes. His hands, thin like Clive's, grasped her fingers in a hearty handshake.

"Lady Danewood," he beamed. "It's hard to imagine anything that could give me greater pleasure than welcoming you to St. Egburt's. Other than having met you soon enough to officiate at your wedding ceremony, of course!"

"We were married by a member of Elizabeth's family in London," said Lord Danewood easily. His bland expression showed no hint of guilt, either for the lie or for his treatment of Clarissa Fanshawe. How had he justified that callous rejection to the Vicar, Elizabeth wondered? She watched Lord Danewood as he smiled again to the Vicar. "We shall promise to hold *all* the Christenings at St. Egburt's," he said.

Mr. Hodge returned his laughter. "You're causing your good lady to blush, my dear sir. There's hardly been time to think of the blessings of a family. Well, well. Do not stand around in this chill breeze, for we don't want Lady Danewood catching cold. That wouldn't be a happy introduction to this lovely part of the country."

He bowed to Elizabeth, politely including David Vincent in his gesture. "My wife and I are looking forward to joining you for luncheon. She will be along directly, I'm sure. We are grateful to you for extending an invitation so soon after your arrival in Berkshire."

Elizabeth managed a tiny smile. "It's my pleasure," she said. "Will you excuse me?" She walked quickly to their waiting carriage, relieved to find that she had still had the strength to cover the short distance unaided.

Brothers, of course. This Mr. Hodge had to be Clive's brother. She pulled at the seams of her gloves, poking unconsciously at a tiny tear in the kid. There was no reason to suppose that her deception was about to be discovered, she told herself. Mr. Adolphus Hodge had never yet visited his brother in Barclay Manor. Perhaps they weren't friends. Perhaps they didn't even write to one another.

She wasn't comforted by her own reassurances. She shuddered as she imagined the consequences if her father ever did discover her whereabouts and learned what she was doing. At least she would have no fear that Clive Hodge would insist on renewing his proposal of marriage. He was more likely to recommend imprisoning her in a dark room, on a permanent diet of bread and water.

Lord Danewood returned to the carriage, interrupting her unpleasant train of thought. She felt a spurt of anger that he could look so unconcerned when it was his scheming that had placed her in such an invidious position. She could sense his disapproval and she fixed her eyes on the distant turret of the church so that she wouldn't have to see the harsh lines etched from his flaring nostrils down to his tautened lips.

He scarcely waited for the coach doors to be shut before he spoke.

"You will now be good enough to explain to me just why you snubbed the Vicar, who is probably one of the kindest and best men I know."

There was no point in pretending that nothing was wrong. "Mr. Hodge reminded me of somebody I know," she said. "My memories of this...this other person are not pleasant ones."

"I don't consider that an adequate reason for insulting an old and respected friend," Lord Danewood replied. "I advise you to overcome these unpleasant memories before Mr. and Mrs. Hodge join us for luncheon. They are good people who strive unceasingly for the welfare of the villagers and I don't intend their one relaxing meal of the week to be made uncomfortable by your decision to indulge in a fit of the sulks."

She swallowed a lump of despair that seemed permanently settled in her throat. "Couldn't I be excused from lunch? There are...good...reasons which make it difficult for me to seem as welcoming as I should to the Vicar."

"I can think of none," said Lord Danewood. "If you care to confide in me, we can consider the matter. Otherwise I expect you to correct the impression you created outside church today. I don't expect my wife to cause embarrassment to my friends."

"Oh no!" exclaimed Elizabeth, taking refuge in anger. "*You* may scandalize the entire neighbourhood with your rejection of Clarissa Fanshawe, but I must be a pattern-card of perfection! That, after all, is only right. A man may do as he chooses but a woman must not only be perfect, she must be *seen* to be perfect."

"Precisely," he said coldly. "Your services have been bought and paid for, Elizabeth. See that you behave appropriately during lunch."

"You're expecting rather a lot from a woman with my background!" she exclaimed, goaded beyond discretion.

"Your background!" he muttered. "What is the truth about that interesting subject, I wonder? Are you really running away from some village scandal as you would have me believe? Or were you carefully trained by Madam Portunio to drive some fool of a man to the brink of madness? That seems more likely, I think."

"I am whatever you wish me to be," she said wearily. His accusing words pricked the bubble of her false anger. "I shall attend your luncheon and be all smiles, my lord. Just do me the favour of turning the conversation away from the subject of my family and my past. I have endured a surfeit of lies in recent weeks."

"Don't worry. I have no desire to expose the sordid details of your past. My plans call for other topics of conversation at the luncheon table."

"Plans? What plans?"

He didn't answer her directly. "You've been brought to Danewood for a purpose. It's time to move forward. Please remember how I expect you to behave at lunch. We're home now, so there is no time for further discussion."

The carriage halted at the marble steps of Danewood Hall. She didn't even pretend to wait and see Lord Danewood assisted from the coach, but hurried into the house, longing for the privacy of her own rooms.

She had dreaded the luncheon so much that the reality was at first nowhere near as grim as her imaginings. Mrs. Hodge, a thin, jolly woman with shrewd brown eyes and a face lined with years of work and laughter, greeted her with a warm cheeriness that calmed Elizabeth's lacerated nerves.

"I'm sorry that we didn't meet at church," said Mrs. Hodge. "My poor little Tom has come down with a toothache and he was too miserable to leave. He seems more comfortable now. Cook made him a brew full of cloves."

"Little Tom!" exclaimed Mr. Hodge teasingly. "I must tell you, Lady Danewood, that little Tom is six feet tall and seventeen years old! But he knows how to wrap the whole household round his capable thumbs."

"Well, he is the only one left at home," said Mrs. Hodge comfortably, as if this explained everything.

Neither the Vicar nor Lord Danewood seemed to find it strange that Mrs. Hodge gave precedence to her son's toothache over attendance in church. Elizabeth wondered what Sir William Barclay and Mr. Clive Hodge would have to say about such a system of priorities. Nevertheless, she soon relaxed under Mrs. Hodge's benevolent gaze and the quiet good sense of the Vicar's conversation. She was amazed to discover halfway through the first course that she was actually enjoying the meal. She noticed that David Vincent was unusually silent, but she didn't struggle to include him in the light-hearted chatter. David's nature was not given to frivolous conversation, she realised.

"Roderick's branch railway line is due to open next month," he said suddenly. His words fell into one of the small silences that can occur at any gathering.

"The lawyers have cleared up the last objections?" Mr. Hodge asked, turning toward Lord Danewood.

"Yes," he replied. "Passenger and freight trains will be running daily into Reading."

"Well, at least it's settled," said Mrs. Hodge. "Now you can pursue your plans for attracting new industry, my lord. It is certainly needed."

"Half the village is starving," said David. "But still you won't accept that it was criminal folly to sell off that land to railway speculators."

Mr. Hodge spoke with gentle reproof. "We know your attachment to Danewood, Mr. Vincent, and to the ways established by your grandfather. But the villagers on Lord Danewood's estate have never gone hungry. Their pride has suffered, perhaps, because they have accepted charity. That is why Lord Danewood was so frustrated by his long illness. It prevented him from seeking the new industry this part of the country so urgently needs. That, thankfully, is now a problem of the past. Under Lady Danewood's influence, we can all see the improvements in Lord Danewood's health and strength."

David dropped his eyes to his food in evident confusion.

"Forgive me. I didn't intend to introduce controversial subjects at Lady Danewood's table."

Lord Danewood stretched out his hand, seeking his glass of wine. Sam unobtrusively guided his master's fingers to close around the thin crystal stem. The valet was a superb actor, Elizabeth thought. She had to keep reminding herself that he knew as well as she did that Lord Danewood was quite capable of seeing his own wineglass. Lord Danewood broke the slight tension engendered by David's remarks.

"My wife and I have some news of a cheerful nature to counteract all this gloom." He raised his glass in a brief gesture of salutation. Elizabeth could just imagine the taunting grey light that would be gleaming in his eyes behind the dark glasses. With her intuitive understanding of his feelings, she knew that David Vincent's remarks had precipitated this sudden intervention. She wished that she didn't have this disconcerting ability to read his moods. It kept her on constant tenterhooks. He smiled blandly to the assembled company.

"Although it's early days to make an announcement of this nature, I would like you three to be the first people to know that our family is soon to be blessed by the addition of a child. Elizabeth is hoping for a Danewood heir, aren't you, my love? But I confess that I'm secretly hoping for a daughter who is as charming as her mother."

The Vicar broke into the surprised silence that followed Lord Danewood's remarks. Elizabeth herself was beyond speech. "So *that* is why you looked pale during the service today, my dear Lady Danewood. I noticed when delivering my sermon that you seemed quite distraught and I really didn't think my message was sufficiently awesome to strike the colour from the cheeks of my listeners!"

Mrs. Hodge smiled affectionately at her husband, before raising her wineglass in a gesture of congratulation. "It's certainly my pleasure to offer you our good wishes for the coming happy event, Lady Danewood. When may we expect the arrival of the little one?"

A piece of bread in Elizabeth's fingers broke into a dozen tiny crumbs, her mind a hopeless blank. When were she and Lord Danewood supposed to have married? "I am n-not sure of the precise date," she said lamely.

"At the end of September," interjected Lord Danewood. "We know that it is to be in September, do we not, my love?"

"Yes," said Elizabeth. Of course, they were supposed to have married in January. Some imp of malice prompted her to add. "I hope there will be time for us to take our wedding journey. We had planned to visit Rome and Athens, you know."

David Vincent looked up quickly from his half-eaten dessert. It occurred to Elizabeth that he looked almost as ill at ease as she was feeling. "I didn't know that you were planning a wedding-journey," he said. "Is that wise in your...er ...delicate condition?"

"Oh, my wife comes from sturdy stock," said Lord Danewood, and his complacent smile was almost convincing enough to deceive Elizabeth. She could feel David's eyes slip with hypnotic fascination to the slimness of her waist. Lord Danewood was going to have to arrange for their "wedding" journey with considerable speed if he wanted to avoid awkward explanations about her slim figure. Unless he was prepared to draw Janet and the other maids into the deception, she couldn't pretend to be gaining non-existent inches.

"Well, well," said the Vicar, sighing contentedly

as he helped himself to a modest portion of pudding, "I'm delighted to learn that it is a gift of God and not the dire effect of my sermon which caused you such discomfort in church this morning."

Elizabeth, grateful for the chance to change the topic of conversation, spoke with unfeigned warmth. "Your sermon was everything which is kind, Mr. Hodge. I have listened to too many lectures on the terrors of Hell. It was pleasant to hear something about the rewards waiting for the virtuous, even if we sometimes fear that we're more likely to be condemned with the goats than rewarded with the sheep."

Mrs. Hodge smiled approvingly. "I'm in complete agreement with your point of view, Lady Danewood. I don't believe the people of our parish are one bit more wicked than people elsewhere, but my husband has to put up with constant accusations that he doesn't scold his flock with sufficient vigour."

"Now, now, my love. You're allowing wifely partiality to overstate the case." Mr. Hodge's affectionate glance removed all sting from his mild reproof. He turned to Elizabeth with a slight shrug of the shoulders. "Lord Danewood has already heard many stories about my younger brother. He is a good man, no doubt, but his view of the Christian ministry is different from my own. I am quite content to follow my path and leave him to follow his, but he feels that it's his duty to try and make me more orthodox."

Mrs. Hodge couldn't contain her indignation. "Orthodox!" she snorted. "If it's sinful to smile then Clive Hodge is certainly orthodox. I don't recall where it's stated that we must make every-body miserable in order to achieve salvation!"

"We have to be tolerant of his disposition at the moment, my dear. You must remember that he has just lost the chance of marrying the woman to whom he had given his heart."

Lord Danewood's hand knocked against the decanter of wine and his head jerked towards Elizabeth. "I hadn't heard this story before," he said to Mr. Hodge. "Your brother holds the living in the village of Barclay, if I recall."

"Yes. And the lady whom he wished to marry is the daughter of his patron. He didn't tell us exactly what happened. Do you remember her name, my love?"

Elizabeth held her breath until Mrs. Hodge shook her head. "Your brother didn't mention it in his letter."

Elizabeth broke into the conversation before the Vicar could say anything more. "Tell me, Mrs. Hodge, what success has the parish enjoyed in establishing a Sunday School for the village children? Do most of them attend school during the week?"

She didn't hear the reply Mrs. Hodge made. She sensed that David Vincent was looking at her with heightened curiosity, but she could do nothing to distract his attention. It was all she could do to sit in her chair, nodding and smiling in what she hoped were appropriate places.

She felt physically sick with relief when she heard David Vincent interject some remark about the drainage project underway on the northern boundary of the estate. She had no idea how the conversation had arrived at such a subject, and she sank back into her seat, unable to pretend that she was listening. She closed her eyes and then heard Lord Danewood's voice cutting sharply down the length of the table.

"We have all finished, Elizabeth, and are waiting for you to withdraw."

She stood up, quite sure she was looking sufficiently pallid to lend credence to her excuses. "I feel a little faint...and I haven't been listening as carefully as I should. Would you all excuse me? Perhaps it's fortunate that you know our news. You will all understand why I am feeling...."

She allowed her voice to tail off into weakness. At least Lord Danewood's lies had provided her with a perfect excuse for fleeing from the table.

Lord Danewood pretended to smile, but she was only reminded of a wolf licking its lips before falling upon its prey. "Certainly you should rest, my dear. I shall make sure nobody disturbs you for several hours. But I shall come up this evening to see how you're feeling. *Nothing,* I can assure you, will keep me from your side tonight."

He smiled at her again, relishing the subtle ironies of a speech which meant one thing to their guests and quite another to her. She managed to make a final polite apology to the Hodges and produced a small smile for David. He, at least, was too courteous to bombard her with difficult questions.

She paused by Lord Danewood's chair on her way out of the dining-room. "Perhaps we can spend the evening planning our wedding trip," she said. "We both know how important it is for *that* journey to be made."

His wolfish expression deepened instead of disappearing. "Oh, I don't know if we should go, my dear. Unless you can overcome these attacks of faintness, perhaps I shall have to insist upon keeping you here. For your own protection, of course."

She couldn't tolerate any more of such cat-and-mouse taunting.

"I must be excused," she said abruptly and fled to the temporary security of her bedroom.

TEN

Elizabeth's heart sank at the sound of Lord Dane-wood's voice in the hall outside her rooms. She heard the door of her sitting-room click shut and watched nervously as Lord Danewood strode towards her, ripping the unnecessary spectacles from his eyes. She thought fleetingly that he had been easier to deal with when he had kept up the pretence of blindness.

He didn't bother to give her any greeting. "Sir William Barclay is your father," he said flatly, not asking a question but simply stating an indisputable fact.

She had planned to deny the relationship, hoping that she still might conceal her past from him, but she had only to take one look at his uncompromising expression to know that lying would be futile.

"Yes," she said. "He is my father."

"And Clive Hodge wanted to marry you?"

"Yes."

There was no outburst of angry words from Lord Danewood. His expression was hard to read but she thought that anger was the emotion furthest from him.

"Oh God!" he exclaimed at last. "How the devil did you end up at Madam Portunio's? I suppose you were running away from Sir William."

"You're not angry?" She couldn't disguise her surprise.

His mouth twisted in self-disgust. "Is that what you expected?" he asked. "Have I been that much of a brute to you?" He turned her chin up towards him, his eyes resting briefly on her parted lips before searching her flushed face with grim intensity. "Why should I be angry with *you*? It was perfectly obvious from the beginning of this misbegotten escapade that you were as innocent of the world as anybody can be once they have left the cradle. I simply preferred to ignore the evidence in front of me. And now, as my old nanny says, I find that I've been so sharp that I've cut myself."

She tried to break the intensity of his mood. "Does your nanny still dare to speak to you with such frankness? Brave woman!"

"She isn't a woman to be over impressed by the mere passage of a few years and the inheritance of a title." Lord Danewood smiled wryly before adding, "You have met her, in fact. Mrs. Smithers, who watched over you in London, was once nurse to me and to my sister. During the time you and I were together in London she often told me, and

167

at great length, that I was making a bad mistake in pretending to marry you."

Elizabeth fought against an inexplicable urge to take Lord Danewood into her arms and comfort him. She didn't enjoy seeing him beset by doubts. She hadn't realised until now just how much she relished the strange excitement of their quarrels. She placed her hands within the warmth of his clasp, not bothering to ask herself why she wanted to feel the strength of his fingers holding her, caressing the pulses at her wrists.

"It wasn't so terrible. Just think what would have happened to me if I had stayed at Madam Portunio's."

He gave a cynical laugh, but his hands tightened around hers. "Are you now casting me in the role of your saviour? Your kindness—or your folly—passes all bounds."

"I'm not silly enough to endow you with virtues you don't possess. But I have reason to be grateful to you since I don't want to go back to Barclay Manor."

"While you are in a confiding mood, would you tell me exactly why you ran away? Was there nobody in your household who could have helped you?"

Elizabeth turned away, not wanting to think about her mother after so many weeks of separation. "You have probably guessed the whole story," she said. "My father was forcing me to marry Mr. Clive Hodge and my mother knew of no way to stop him. She was frightened at the prospect of sending me to London, but it seemed to me that no fate could be worse than a lifetime tied to Mr. Hodge." She smiled tentatively. "I suppose you could say that I'm a wiser woman now."

Lord Danewood didn't respond to her attempt at humour. "It's my duty to take you back to Barclay Manor immediately," he said.

"Oh no! *Please* don't send me back, my lord!"

"It's my responsibility to help you to salvage what we can of this wreckage of your reputation. I have dragged you into this mess, I must help you to get out."

"We both know that I'm ruined, my lord. Why punish me by returning me to Barclay Manor? You can't begin to imagine what my life was like there. I won't go back. I *can't*."

"God knows I have no wish to send you away. I need you here." He jerked his head away from her and walked across the room to the hearth. "If only we had been more discreet in disclosing your true name."

"You mean that I can stay here?"

"I shall leave the decision up to you. But first I must tell you honestly what has been going on at Danewood. Will you sit with me by the fire while I try to explain why I would like you to stay?"

She went willingly—far too willingly—and curled up on a cushion at Lord Danewood's feet. Sir William Barclay and Clive Hodge seemed a long way away, dim figures from an unreal past. She felt at peace sitting in front of the fire, watching the orange flicker of its dying embers.

Lord Danewood's voice when he finally spoke was so calm that it was a few seconds before she realised how effectively his words had shattered the tranquil atmosphere of the room.

"Somebody has been trying to murder me for more than a year, ever since I became betrothed to Clarissa Fanshawe, in fact. The first attempt was a clumsy effort to destroy a small bridge I use in riding from the Hall to the village. The fire in the stables was the second attempt. You will remember that I have already mentioned the third attempt to you. My sleeping-draught was poisoned."

She sat quite still for a second, while the meaning of his words sank in, then she jumped up. She rejected his words instinctively, determined to deny a possibility she found too horrible to accept.

"But the fire was an accident!" she cried. "Everyone is agreed upon the fact. And the poison... You mustn't rely upon impressions you formed at a time when you were only partly conscious."

He placed his hands on her shoulders, forcing her to look up at him. "Do I seem to you to be a man much given to imagining plots against his life?"

When she didn't answer him, he said more gently, "The fire in the stables is considered an accident because that is how I described it. But, in reality, I spotted smoke coming from one of the stalls when I was out riding late at night. When I rode up to investigate, somebody knocked me over the head. I was only unconscious for a minute or two, but whoever hit me wrapped a sack over my head, so that I couldn't identify my attacker. My would-be murderer dragged me to the door of the tack-room and then dropped a heavy saddle over my head as though it had fallen from a burning hook. The blow from the saddle knocked me out completely for a while, although not for long enough. The murderer was determined that the fire should appear an accident, so he had not set the horses free from their stalls. I shall remember the screams of the animals and the frantic noise of their hooves against the wooden walls until the day I die."

"It is...horrible..." whispered Elizabeth. "Thank God Sam was able to rescue you."

"Yes. Sam's bravery must have been a severe blow to the murderer."

"But who could possibly wish to do such a thing, my lord? Why should anybody wish you dead?"

Lord Danewood's expression twisted with new bitterness. "I can think of a number of people who would profit from my death. For example, the railway has already put paid to the coach service which operated between here and Reading. Three of the local posting inns closed down because of lack of road traffic. I personally closed a cloth factory because it was too small and old-fashioned to compete with the mills in the North. Many of my estate workers are unemployed, and when men are out of work, they will contemplate desperate measures. They also know that David Vincent, who is the heir to Danewood, would pursue very different policies from mine."

"But you'll find your labourers new work soon, won't you?"

"I have already promised to train everybody who finds himself without work, but it's easy to stir up agitation among people who are uneducated and who see dire poverty all around them. The Civil War in America has thrown half of Lancashire out of work because of shortage of cotton, and rumours of starvation travel fast. One hot-head can convince an entire village that it will soon be starving. I know someone is stirring up my workers. I just don't know who."

"The village seemed so peaceful when David took me there."

Lord Danewood sighed. "David and Mr. and Mrs. Hodge have worked wonders in finding odd jobs and relieving the worst cases of hardship. What we need, however, is a long-term solution. I am trying to establish new industry here, but my plans were badly delayed after the fire. I was ill for far too many weeks, and this continuing pretence of blindness doesn't help."

Her voice betrayed her bewilderment. "Then throw off this pretence, my lord, and establish your new industries! Why all this need for deception?"

Lord Danewood stared into the depths of the dying fire.

"If only I could be certain that the attacks originated in the village... The stable fire could easily have been the work of a villager, but the broken bridge was only effective if somebody knew precisely when I was going to ride across it. And I want to know who bribed the nurse to poison me. Somebody, you know, hustled her out of Danewood before I could question her. Was that done by an unemployed villager? Nobody in Danewood will admit to knowing when she left or where she went, and I dare not press my enquiries too closely or it will arouse suspicions. In London I tried to trace her, but I found out she wasn't sent from the agency which was supposed to have supplied her."

"Are you suggesting that some servant inside

Danewood Hall is conspiring with the villagers to murder you? They all seem to admire you and your managment of the estate."

His expression was wry. "You can hardly expect the would-be murderer to sneak around the house, scowling every time he sees me. Ah, Elizabeth! Your face is too revealing. I can see that you still believe these attacks are figments of my over-active imagination. But *I* can't forget the fact that I'm a very wealthy man without children or a wife to inherit my wealth. The Danewood legacy is a very tempting one, my dear."

She looked up quickly and caught his rueful expression. "Yes," he said. "That was the reason for my sudden announcement that you are to have a child. That was why I arranged our pretended marriage. If people believe I have a wife, they will also believe that she is heir to most of my estate."

"I see," said Elizabeth quietly. "Playing your wife is rather a dangerous role, my lord."

Lord Danewood's cheeks lost all vestige of colour. "You have every right to be angry with me. It's true that Clarissa Fanshawe no longer wanted to marry me. But I arranged a false marriage precisely because I didn't want to expose any true wife of mine to the risks of becoming Lady Danewood."

"You considered me expendable, in other words."

Quickly he reached out to touch her. "Never that. Sam and I have watched over you from the moment you set foot in Danewood."

Her body still ached to rest against his knees despite the revelations he had made. Deliberately she moved away from him, so that her mind could be free to think. "Your plotting hasn't been very successful. Here you sit, alive and unharmed. There hasn't been any attempt to make another attack."

Lord Danewood spoke carefully, watching her angry face.

"What you say is true. I thought a helpless, blind victim might tempt the murderer into being careless. But in fact my assailant seems to have become more cautious. That is why I went to London. I wanted to find out if some organized labour group was responsible for the wild rumours that keep surfacing among my unemployed men. Most of all, I hoped that by returning with a wife, I would spur my enemy into indiscretion. But it seems my ploy has failed, because there has been nothing. That's why I announced today that we are expecting a child."

"How is that going to help?"

The tension in Lord Danewood's face belied the calm of his voice. "Most of the estate is entailed, and it's well-known that David Vincent believes in a return to the traditional methods of managing an estate. If he inherited Danewood, life here would certainly be very different for many people. Some villagers certainly believe life would be better. We can safely assume, I think, that my killer wanted David to inherit the estate. Now I have announced that you are expecting my child and I imagine there's a good chance that the killer will turn his attentions to you. There's no point in disposing of me if you are about to produce an heir to follow on in my footsteps. My lawyers have been given strict instructions about how the estate is to be run during the minority of my heir."

She sprang to her feet. "Now I *know* that your

illness has left you unhinged! I'm supposed to provide a sitting target for a homicidal lunatic! Do you expect me to believe all your outrageous stories and then sit back, waiting calmly for my execution?"

He stood up and took her angry face gently between his hands. "You are confused, I think. If I have been telling you lies, then there's no danger from any mysterious murderer. If you think you are in danger then you must also accept that I'm speaking rationally. Which is it to be, Elizabeth? Do you think I'm mad? Or do you think I'm callous, lacking in concern for your welfare but nevertheless speaking the truth?"

She twisted out of his clasp. She needed to remove herself from such close contact or she would find herself agreeing to become the bait in Lord Danewood's trap. She deliberately goaded herself to anger. "When you express your question in such a way, my lord, the answer is easy. I have no difficulty in believing you to be utterly callous. Entirely without feeling for me, in fact. Perhaps I should be grateful that you bothered to warn me of my fate! Did you expect me to express my appreciation for your kindly gesture in informing me that I'm likely to be pursued by a mad killer?"

He laughed briefly. "I know you too well by now. I certainly didn't expect your thanks. In fact, I came to your room anticipating exactly what has transpired—fireworks!"

"But I've no doubt you expected to charm me into agreement one way or another."

Lord Danewood raised a quizzical eyebrow. "I didn't realise that I possessed any charm as far as you were concerned. I wouldn't dream of persuad-

175

ing you against your will. You have every right to insist upon being taken back to Barclay Manor. But if you do agree to stay, you will want to know what precautions I have taken to ensure your safety. My old nurse, Mrs. Smithers, has already arrived from London and she is ready to take on the task of protecting you, just as Sam protects me. She will sleep in your bedroom from now on, and during the day you are forbidden to leave the house alone. You must tell me each morning exactly what you plan to do, and where you plan to go, and I shall tell Janet that she is to keep an eye on you at all times. We can use the excuse of your pregnancy. I shall tell Janet that you have become susceptible to fainting fits, and she is responsible for knowing where you are at all times."

"That won't work," said Elizabeth. "If I'm too well protected, then the murderer will not dare to proceed with his attempt to remove me."

"Well, the murderer won't know about these precautions. Besides, I am going to make sure that he becomes desperate enough to take the risk. Tomorrow I'm going to announce to the world that my eyes have become sensitive to vague impressions of light and movement. I shall prepare for a trip back to the specialists in London. You will prepare to come with me. If all this doesn't spur my would-be villain to action, then I shall have to accept that my suspicions were the product of a sick mind. Do you think, on these terms, that you could agree to help me?"

She had known all along, of course, that she would do whatever he asked. When he held her within the circle of his arms she could deny him nothing. She tried to make her voice sound light, as if she had agreed to a mere trifle. "Since I have quite set my heart on seeing Rome and Athens, I suppose I shall have to fall in with your wishes. Why should I worry about a few more days at Danewood when, according to you, I have already survived several weeks under the nose of a homicidal lunatic?"

"Thank you," he said simply, although his arms tightened compulsively around her. Almost against his will, it seemed that his gaze fastened on her parted lips and he bent his head to kiss her.

"My lord!" They heard Sam's low voice through the panels of the door. "My lord! You must come at once. There has been another accident. Mr. Vincent is hurt."

Lord Danewood released Elizabeth from his arms. "Stay here, and don't open your door to anyone, do you understand?"

"Oh yes! Hurry, Roderick! I didn't wish for such dramatic proof of your suspicions."

"I don't understand it," muttered Lord Danewood. "It *must* be an accident."

"My lord!" Sam's voice was increasingly frantic. "He's bleeding something fearful, my lord."

"Your dark spectacles, Roderick!" she called out as he strode hastily towards the door.

"I think it's time for my sight to start improving," he said grimly. "Remember what I told you. Lock the door behind me and don't open it to anybody until I return."

ELEVEN

Elizabeth placed a gentle hand on David Vincent's forehead. It was cool, without a trace of fever, and she sighed with relief. She wished, though, that he would wake from his overlong sleep. Surely it could not be a healthy sign that he was taking so long to regain consciousness?

As if in answer to her silent worries, he stirred restlessly against the soft, white pillows and his eyes flickered open to rest upon her face.

"What has happened?" His voice was a mere thread of sound, and she could feel his pulse beginning to race.

"There was a slight accident," she said. "But you have suffered no real hurt, thank God."

A ghost of a smile altered the sickly cast of his face.

"I shall take your word for it, Cousin. If I'm unhurt, could you please explain why my head feels as though somebody is beating it with a fair-sized hammer?"

Elizabeth smiled. It was good to see that David was feeling strong enough to joke about his condition. She picked up the doctor's draught of medicine, trying to decide what to ask him about his accident.

"We were hoping *you* could tell *us* what happened," she said at last. "We think, perhaps, you fell down the servants' stairs. Sam discovered you lying at the foot of the staircase in a pool of blood."

David shook his head, wincing at the pain of the sudden movement. "Why was I using the servants' stairs?"

"Perhaps you will remember everything later on." She certainly hoped that he would. Danewood Hall didn't need any more unexplained accidents. "The doctor assured us that although the graze on your head *looks* very messy, the wound is only on the surface of your scalp. We were worried at first in case you had suffered a severe concussion, but Dr. Small said you would come round during the night. You have tossed and turned a great deal since he left, keeping us in suspense for several hours."

"What time is it now?"

"It's the middle of the morning. Mrs. Smithers watched over you during the night and I have been here since breakfast." She smiled as she poured the draught of medicine from the doctor's bottle into a tall glass. "I've been left with strict instructions to see that you drink all of this. I expect it will help to muffle those hammers inside your head!"

David wrinkled his nose. "Faugh! I can smell

how disgusting it's going to taste. And when I've been virtuous and swallowed that, I suppose you'll insist upon feeding me a breakfast of thin gruel?"

"Perhaps we might risk thick gruel since you're showing such rapid powers of recovery!" She sat down on the bed and raised his head to sip the medicine. "Let me ring for your valet and I'll return later on to find out what I can do to cheer you up during your stay in bed."

"You're so good, Elizabeth. I hate to impose on your nursing time, when your hands must already be full with your other invalid."

She paused with her hands on the bellpull, her expression blank. "Nobody else was injured, David. What do you mean?"

He fell back against the pillows, his eyes closing. "Forgive me. Of course you don't think of Roderick as an invalid. You are accustomed to his blindness. I, however, remember him as he once was."

She was tempted to tell him that Lord Danewood was no invalid, but rather a man at the height of his powers. She decided against it. This wasn't the moment to burden David with news about his cousin's recovery from blindness. She was glad that David's valet responded quickly to her summons, and saved her from making a direct reply.

"Will you send a message to my rooms when your master is ready to eat breakfast? I will bring it to him myself."

She left with a final encouraging smile for David.

Janet was waiting for her when she returned to her rooms.

"I think I'll take a bath, Janet." The hours of anxious waiting by David's bedside had proved more physically tiring than she had anticipated.

"Yes, m'lady." The maid started to walk sedately into the dressing-room, then turned back again with an impetuous exclamation. "Oh, my lady! We're so happy for you. It seems as though everything is going to turn out right at Danewood again."

"What do you mean, Janet?"

"We've heard the news about his lordship's eyes. And then to learn about...about your ladyship's condition. We know we shouldn't have gossiped in the servants' hall, but we're all that thrilled we hardly know how to set about doing our work. Seems you've brought a breath of sunshine after all these dark months. 'Tis too good to be true, that's what we all said, m'lady."

"Too good to be true, indeed," murmured Elizabeth. She glanced up and saw the maid's excited face. "Thank you for your good wishes, Janet." She wondered how Lord Danewood would break the news to his servants that his "wife" had died abroad and there wasn't going to be any Danewood heir. That, thank heavens, was not her problem.

"Perhaps you could see about the water for my bath," she said, feeling too weary to cope any longer with the complexities of life at Danewood.

She had scarcely dressed in fresh clothes and settled down to eat her own breakfast, when there was a brief knock at the door. She was amazed to see David Vincent, his eyes wild in a stark white face, lurch through the doorway. Instantly, she sprang to her feet.

"*David!* How could your valet let you out of bed?

181

Come and lie down here at once." She hastened to force him down on the couch in her sitting-room, running into the bedroom to pull a cover off her bed and tucking it round his shivering form.

He grabbed her hand with astonishing strength. "Roderick's eyes!" He ground the words out through a mouth that seemed clenched tight with pain. "Is it true what the valet tells me? Roderick can see again?"

She struggled to remove her wrist and he became aware of the fact that he had seized her. He dropped her hand as though it seared his fingers, his face flaming as he muttered an apology. She touched her hand to his forehead and found it burning with heat.

"David, you must calm down. If I had known the effect the news would have upon you, I would have forbidden the servants to speak of it until you were stronger."

"But is it true? Can he see?"

"Yes, it's true. Roderick believes he may be regaining his sight, although his power of vision isn't fully restored."

She didn't want to elaborate on the lie, or to get herself more deeply enmeshed in false descriptions of Lord Danewood's cure. She felt uncomfortable at deceiving somebody who had proved himself a staunch friend. If his health had not seemed so uncertain, she would have told him something about Lord Danewood's terrible suspicions. She disapproved, now that she thought about it, of Lord Danewood's treatment of his cousin. He had never taken David into his confidence. He had gone out of his way, in fact, to avoid telling David the truth about his eyes.

At her words, David fell back on the sofa, his breath expelling in a great sigh. "Forgive me, Elizabeth, for bursting in here. I couldn't credit my valet's news. It has been so long... We had almost given up hope... What a relief to know that Danewood will soon be returned to the charge of its true master!"

"There is still a long way to go before your cousin is declared well enough to run Danewood again, David. And even then, he won't be able to manage without your help. I have often heard him say so." She saw that the flattering remarks had soothed him somewhat, and the hectic flush on his cheeks faded. She hoped this justified her lie, since in reality Lord Danewood had never discussed David's abilities with her.

Janet returned at that moment, stopping short at the sight of Mr. Vincent spread-eagled on her mistress's couch.

"Oh! Has there been another accident, m'lady?" she cried out.

"No," Elizabeth replied quickly. "Mr. Vincent wished to speak with me and over-estimated his own strength. He'll need help to get back to his own room." She turned back to David and said, only half-teasing.

"You must promise me to stay in bed, or I shall bring Sam upstairs to look after you. I don't think you'd spring past *his* restraining arms as easily as you escaped your valet."

He smiled ruefully. "I was almost delirious with joy when I heard about Roderick. But I'll promise to remain quietly in my bed until the doctor says I may leave it."

Elizabeth smothered a sigh of relief. For a few

minutes she had wondered if David was actually walking about in a delirium, his manner had been so far removed from normal.

"I shall ring for Sam, my lady," Janet announced in tones that brooked no argument. "Sam and I will escort Mr. Vincent back to his own bedroom. His lordship is waiting for you to join him downstairs. It's almost lunchtime."

"So late! I hadn't realised." She stretched out her hands to David in a gesture of affection. "Hurry off to bed, dear Cousin, for that's the quickest way to recover, you know."

David had regained his usual polite manner. "Enjoy your luncheon with Roderick. Think of me struggling with my bowl of gruel!"

In the end, David was declared fit to leave his bed on the very next day. He immediately announced that he needed to return to Greystones, his own modest estate inherited from his mother. Urgent business there, he said, had been awaiting his attention for over two weeks.

Dr. Small finally agreed that it was better to allow him to travel and take care of the business that appeared to be worrying him. Patients suffering from minor head injuries needed to be worry-free, declared the doctor, tut-tutting at the rate of David's pulse. "Too bad we're past the days of blood-letting, Mr. Vincent. A few leeches would soon put paid to all this hare-brained scampering about the countryside."

David bore up reasonably well under such paternal chafing and left Danewood with promises to Elizabeth that he would soon be returning. She was surprised at how much she missed his presence. With David she felt relaxed, almost motherly, whereas with Lord Danewood she was invariably on tenterhooks, mistrusting herself at least as much as she mistrusted him.

It was almost a relief to wake up on a bright, warm morning and discover that it was Sunday once again. The days were slipping by unmarred by even a hint of violence. Before long, Elizabeth thought, Lord Danewood would have to admit that he had allowed his imagination to run away with his commonsense. He had survived three unfortunate accidents, not three murderous attacks.

She got ready for the Morning Service with a cheerfulness she wouldn't have believed possible only the week before. By concentrating her attention upon the pleasant subject of which gloves to choose and which bonnet to tie over her chestnut curls, she managed to avoid any uncomfortable crisis of conscience.

Janet fussed over her, wrapping her shoulders with unnecessary shawls and the butler himself handed her solicitously into the crested carriage. It was difficult to remember that this smiling man, beaming at her with avuncular approval, was the same disapproving ogre who had greeted her arrival at Danewood Hall. Lord Danewood's servants, she thought peevishly, were certainly anxious to see him reproduce himself. Her startling rise in domestic favour coincided precisely with the announcement of her interesting position as the mother of the future Danewood heir.

It was only a short distance to the church and she didn't want to spoil the pleasure of their drive, but she couldn't help giving voice to her worries. "What are your servants going to say, my lord, when you have to tell them that I'm dead and there is going to be no Danewood heir?"

Lord Danewood was silent. "I no longer consider your supposed death a very satisfactory conclusion to this affair," he said at last. "Perhaps, after the service, we should discuss our plans for the future. We can't keep up the pretence of my partially-restored sight much longer. I shall soon have to proclaim myself cured. I ought to leave Danewood next week for London because there are projects there waiting for my attention."

"Then let's leave together," she said eagerly. She wanted to leave Danewood before her heart became even more irretrievably lost. "We can take Sam and Mrs. Smithers, since they are the only two servants who know the truth of our situation. We could all four travel to the Continent and eventually you three could arrive back in Danewood carrying the...the news about my death." She faltered slightly before saying, "If you could manage to escort me to Rome, I would appreciate it very much. I don't altogether trust my judgment about finding somewhere to live after the episode with Madam Portunio. My rescue might not come quite so opportunely next time."

"What rescue?" he asked. "Dammit, Elizabeth, I didn't *rescue* you. Don't you realise that you're ruined, and I am at least partly responsible?"

The carriage braked in front of the church porch and she turned away from his questioning gaze. She was certainly ruined, but not for any of the reasons Lord Danewood imagined. The real question was how she would endure living out the rest of her days with a broken heart.

They scarcely had time to descend the carriage

steps, before Mr. Hodge bustled up to them. "I'm so glad to catch you, Danewood, before you entered church. A most mysterious thing has happened and I need your advice, my lord."

"Perhaps we should talk at length after the service. There are several matters...."

Lord Danewood's suggestion was carried no further. His gaze, still masked by the dark spectacles, was transfixed by the arrival of a newcomer upon the scene. It was fortunate that he no longer wished to feign blindness, for he drew in his breath sharply and turned instantly towards Elizabeth, placing his hand firmly, almost roughly, beneath her elbow.

Elizabeth couldn't move. Her gaze was riveted on the approaching visitor. She wanted to turn away, to scream, to flee to the carriage, but her body was bolted to the ground. She could only stare at the thin, stooped figure in hypnotised silence.

"*That* is what I wanted to tell you, Danewood," said Mr. Adolphus Hodge. "My brother was summoned here by an urgent letter...."

Mr. Clive Hodge, who was advancing with the stately deliberation of a triumphant army, paused only inches away from Elizabeth. "Miss Barclay?" he exclaimed. "Miss Barclay! Can my eyes be deceiving me?"

"It seems unlikely," said his brother impatiently. "I gather you have already met Lady Danewood, Clive?"

Clive Hodge ignored the question. "There is the answer to our mystery!" he cried exultantly. "I was summoned by the Lord to be His instrument of retribution. Vengeance is mine, saith the Lord, and I, Clive Hodge, am to be His sturdy Sword of Justice."

"That's all very well," said Adolphus Hodge testily. "But are you seriously suggesting that the Almighty summoned you here by means of the Penny Post?"

Once again, Clive did not deign to respond to his brother, but stared piously at the sky as if searching for some further signal of Divine approval.

Elizabeth looked at her former betrothed's expression of fanatical self-righteousness and tried very hard to faint. Her robust constitution betrayed her, however, and although she turned pale no welcome oblivion reached out to cloak her in darkness.

"R-Roderick...?" She managed to draw out his name on a note of quivering enquiry. He turned to her, his expression apparently one of simple solicitude.

"My love," he said suavely, chiding her gently. "You must remember your delicate condition." He leaned over her with a convincing display of husbandly concern. "Pretend to faint, dammit! I need time to think!"

She obligingly gave a feeble moan before swaying picturesquely into Lord Danewood's embrace.

"Roderick!" she sighed and allowed herself to crumple against him with the full force of her weight. She hoped she looked pale and wan. She was frightened enough to look pretty sickly. What on earth could Lord Danewood do now? Even so influential a personage as he would have trouble outfacing the sort of scandal Clive Hodge was preparing to brew.

She remained limp and languid in Lord Dane-wood's arms as the servants hurried to pull the travelling rugs from the coach. They spread the covers two or three deep on a grassy knoll by the porch and Lord Danewood lowered her tenderly on to the makeshift bed. She wondered if it was time to start reviving—surely this faint had gone on rather too long?—and she opened one tentative eye. Lord Danewood scowled back and she hastily lowered the offending eyelid. Mr. Adolphus Hodge fussed over her, exclaiming in concern and blaming himself for precipitating the attack. She wished that she could reassure him that this was all a pretence. He was too good a man to deceive. He finally scurried away at Lord Danewood's suggestion to conduct Morning Service, saying he would send somebody back with a glass of water.

Clive Hodge, his face twisted into a mask of astonished disbelief, watched all these attentions to the sinful Elizabeth Barclay. His brain was in a whirl of righteous wrath, mixed up with the heady anticipation of vengeance. He could scarcely credit the scenes in front of his own eyes. Nobody gave the slightest indication that they realised they were dealing with a Scarlet Woman. He reflected bitterly that with a pastor like Adolphus it was no wonder the parishioners were so easily beguiled into sin. One glance at Elizabeth's brazen clothes and wicked hairstyle was surely sufficient to convince any virtuous person that here before him stood—or rather lay—the Personification of Satanic Temptation.

Nobody, he noticed, had even bothered to cover her ankles. He stared for several minutes at Eliz-abeth's white silk stockings and lace-trimmed petticoat which could be seen quite clearly beneath the hem of her crinoline. How disgusting that she should be allowed to deck herself out in gowns of pale blue and then flaunt herself before the unsuspecting men of the parish!

His gaze crept up towards Elizabeth's face and he jumped when Lord Danewood suddenly spoke. "She is beginning to come round." He prodded Elizabeth to make sure that she got the point, and obligingly she fluttered her eyelashes and gave a ladylike sigh. "Pray, Mr. Hodge, be good enough to lend your arm in support," she heard Lord Danewood say. "Naturally we must return to Danewood Hall at once."

Clive Hodge had not succeeded in assembling his jumbled thoughts into the coherent denunciation he was seeking.

"But she is Miss Barclay," he stuttered impotently. "She ran away from Barclay Manor."

Elizabeth ventured another feeble sigh and marvelled at the cool note of disdain Lord Danewood managed to inject into his voice.

"Your information concerning my wife's past scarcely comes as news to me, Sir. I would point out to you, however, that this is *not* Miss Barclay. This is Lady Danewood, my wife."

He allowed a few moments of silence for the words to sink in, then he spoke politely, as if the former conversation had never been. "Perhaps, Mr. Hodge, you would be good enough to offer *Lady Danewood* your arm?" The subtle emphasis on Elizabeth's supposed title, hinted that he wouldn't tolerate further remarks concerning Miss Barclay.

She allowed herself to be supported back to the carriage, although she took care not to lean against Clive Hodge. She settled into the corner of the coach and said with feigned apology, "All this fainting, I can't understand it, Roderick. It's so unlike me."

Lord Danewood patted her hand. "But you have never before been in a delicate condition, my love." He sounded so protective that Elizabeth wondered if he could possibly have forgotten that their marriage and her pregnancy were entirely mythical.

Before Clive Hodge could do more than gasp at this fresh piece of news, Lord Danewood had dismissed him with a curt nod.

"Morning Service is well advanced, Sir, and I'm sure you won't want to miss the opportunity to attend to your devotions. Please do come to lunch at Danewood with my friends Mr. and Mrs. Adolphus Hodge. Undoubtedly you will have some recent news concerning the welfare of Lady Danewood's family."

He gave a brisk nod to Sam who, realising the unspoken urgency of the situation, quickly raised the carriage steps and sprang up into his driving seat. Lord Danewood bowed politely to the stranded Mr. Hodge, before leaning back in the carriage.

"And how the devil are we going to get out of this mess?" he asked.

TWELVE

"Surely your capacity for deception hasn't deserted you?" replied Elizabeth tartly. "You have never previously suffered from any lack of powers of invention."

She looked down at her gloved hands, which lay clasped tightly together in her lap. "Oh Roderick! What are we to do? You don't know Clive Hodge. You can't begin to guess at the depths of vindictiveness that lie beneath the pious surface! He will do his best to ruin you, Roderick, if he can."

Lord Danewood looked at her, a curious light glowing in the back of his eyes. "And what of you, Elizabeth? Don't you care if he also ruins you?"

She tried to smile. "Well, as for that, you have already told me at least a hundred times that I'm ruined already. What more can he do, except take me back to Barclay Manor?"

Lord Danewood reached out to still the restless

plucking of her hands. "He couldn't even do that if you would agree to make our marriage a legal fact instead of a piece of make-believe."

His voice was warm and gently caressing, making it all too easy to forget the realities of their position. She wanted to throw herself into his arms, to rest her head on the comforting strength of his shoulders and let him protect her from Clive Hodge and from her father. She knew it was impossible, of course, however tender his voice might sound. She had to stop thinking of her own wishes and try to show him the dangers lying ahead.

"We must work out a *sensible* plan for dealing with Clive Hodge, and quickly. He will create a scandal that will rock St. Egburt's to its foundations. You will be ruined, but he will proceed carelessly on his way, secure in the knowledge that the Lord's will has triumphed."

"You aren't thinking clearly, my love. If we are really married, there is nothing he can do. We must go to London and be married there by special licence." He managed to sound as though marrying Elizabeth was the summit of his ambitions. "Sam and Mrs. Smithers shall be our witnesses and then nobody need ever be any the wiser as to the actual date of the ceremony." His face was twisted by a cynical smile. "Once I have visited your father to inform him of the financial settlements, I doubt if he will have the smallest interest in discussing when the marriage occurred. I am, as I have told you before, a very wealthy man."

She was tempted to fall in with his plan and allow herself to relish the prospect of happiness his words opened up before her. But she retained just sufficient self-control to realise that a marriage based on her opportunism and his generosity was not likely to lead to a lifetime of wedded bliss. She pulled her hand out of his grasp. It was easier to be sensible when his fingers were not sending quivering sensations along the nerve endings of her arm.

"You're generous in offering to protect me," she said. Her voice sounded pinched and prim, but she couldn't help it. "Of course, I can't accept your offer. For one thing, Clive Hodge will soon realise that I could never have met you in time to contract a normal marriage, especially since we're pretending I'm already with child. Clive Hodge knows that we had never met before I ran away from Barclay Manor."

"I think we can use his own prejudices as a weapon against him," said Lord Danewood. "He isn't at all like his brother except for a startling physical resemblance. The Vicar here always looks for the good in people, and he often finds virtue concealed beneath the most unlikely exteriors. Clive Hodge, however, is always looking for evil. If no sin is there, he invents it. He would easily believe that you and I had a clandestine love affair. He would have no difficulty in believing that you ran away so that we could be secretly married. It would even salve his own pride, by explaining to him why you refused *his* offer."

"It's true that Mr. Hodge likes to believe the worst," she agreed. "But you haven't understood what life is like at Barclay Manor, Roderick. Clandestine meetings would have been absolutely impossible."

He smiled slightly. "You think that because you

never tried to arrange any such thing. Did you *never* go out alone?"

"To visit a villager, perhaps, or to carry a message for Papa. But Mama was nearly always with me. If not, I took one of the maids."

"How about riding? Did you never ride alone?"

Elizabeth sat silently for a moment. "Yes," she said finally. "Yes, I sometimes rode alone."

"Then there is our answer!" he exclaimed. "We met last summer before my accident and a violent passion flared immediately between us. Before I could ask for permission to marry you, my accident intervened and I was confined to bed. We can be a little vague as to why you never mentioned my name to your father. Clive Hodge, after all, has no authority over either of us. He can't demand evidence, or even an explanation of our behaviour. And you're forgetting the mysterious letter which brought him here. We shall have a few questions of our own to ask of Mr. Clive Hodge."

"You can't marry me simply because Clive is making difficulties," she said helplessly. "You can't *want* to marry me." She longed for him to disagree. She wanted him to sweep her into his arms and say he loved her. She looked at his harsh features, familiar to her now in every line, and her eyes misted with tears. Was she crazy to reject the chance of marrying this man? What did it matter if he could never love somebody who had caused him so much trouble?

He didn't fulfill her fantasy, of course. He didn't clasp her to him and utter words of eternal devotion. He merely polished his tinted spectacles and said prosaically, "This ought to be a lesson to me. In future I shan't involve innocent people in my convoluted plans. I'm sorry that you're having to pay such a heavy price for my folly, but I shall strive to be a—kind—husband."

"I don't want a kind husband!" she cried, and was thankful when he interrupted her before she could expose the true state of her feelings any further.

"We have arrived at the gates for Danewood. You will only have a short time in your room to freshen your appearance before our guests arrive. You have little enough reason to trust my judgment, Elizabeth, but I beg you to follow my lead in conversation at the luncheon table. Whatever transpires, I can at least console myself with the thought that I shall be a more suitable husband for you than Clive Hodge."

"You must know, Lord Danewood, that you are an exceptionally eligible matrimonial prize. Your wife must inevitably be the envy of most young women in the county."

She was looking out of the carriage window as she spoke so that he wouldn't be able to read the betraying emotions flooding her face, so it was she who spotted the lone horseman ahead of them on the driveway. "Oh look, my lord! David Vincent has returned. How glad I am that he took no serious hurt from his fall!"

Lord Danewood's voice was harsher than she had ever heard it. "I'm well aware that my cousin excites in you all the tender emotions that I fail to arouse," he said curtly. "But since you're shortly to become my wife, I should appreciate it if you could strive to contain your feelings."

She looked at him in astonishment, for his tone suggested a man racked by jealousy. The carriage door swung open at that moment, and she found both Sam and David Vincent waiting to assist her down the steps. She smiled her thanks but Lord Danewood spoke before she could enquire how David was feeling.

"Welcome back, David. You've been luckier with your accident, I see, than I was with mine."

David greeted Elizabeth before replying to his cousin. "The cut is almost healed, I'm thankful to say, although I have occasional headaches which remind me to take care when walking downstairs."

"You still don't remember why you were using the servants' staircase?" asked Lord Danewood.

"No." A worried frown wrinkled David's forehead. "I can't remember why I was there. I have a feeling I received a message...It's fortunate I wasn't carrying a candle or the servants' wing might have gone up in flames. The whole episode remains a mystery."

"Indeed it does," said Lord Danewood smiling affably. "But we shouldn't trouble our heads about it any further." Elizabeth looked up at him quickly, mistrusting the tone of his voice. Before she could speak, David broke into the slight silence with a cheerfulness that had previously been lacking.

"The grooms have already been filling me with good news about your eyes, Roderick. Before I could get down from my horse they were pouring out stories about your improving eyesight. I gather that your vision continues to improve?"

"Yes. It's encouraging, is it not? I think that in good light I could distinguish features clearly enough to recognize any individual. I'm allowing myself to hope for a full recovery."

"How are you responding to these exciting changes, Elizabeth?" David asked.

"I think we should go inside," she said breathlessly, not wanting to expand on Lord Danewood's lies. "I must hurry up and remove my bonnet," she said, glad for once that the female mind wasn't supposed to be able to rise above such trivialities. "Roderick, will you take care of David? I'll see you both at lunch."

She hurried away before either of them could say anything further to add to her discomfort. It had finally dawned on her that Lord Danewood and David Vincent cordially disliked one another and she could only wonder how this insight had been denied to her for so many weeks.

She was ready for lunch and had already dismissed the maid when she heard a knock at the door. "Roderick?" she asked as she started to open it.

David Vincent was standing on the threshold and he gave her a rueful smile. "Not Roderick, I'm afraid, but at least I'm bringing you word from him. There has been a change in our plans for lunch. Mr. and Mrs. Hodge sent an urgent request for Roderick's presence and he has already left for the Vicarage. There wasn't time for him to explain to you precisely what had occurred. He didn't say why they needed him—something to do with Mr. Clive Hodge, I believe. He has asked me to act as your escort and drive you to join him at the Vicarage. We shall eat lunch as guests of the Hodges."

"I see," she said, her brain working feverishly. She could think of only too many reasons why

Lord Danewood might have felt the need to go rushing off to the Vicarage.

"You look upset, Cousin," David said politely, his voice tinged with concern.

She had no intention of enlarging upon her worries about Clive Hodge. David, conventional and restrained as his character was, would be the last man to confide in. "I was thinking about the cook," she lied. "We must send a message to say that after all nobody will be here for lunch." She walked over to the bell-rope, ready to summon one of the maids, but David followed her quickly into the room and prevented her pulling the cord.

"I've already delivered a message to the kitchens," he said. "I guessed that your first thought would be for the inconvenience of the servants."

Now that she was aware of the animosity between Roderick and David Vincent, she couldn't feel entirely relaxed in his company. She moved away from the bell, uncomfortable at the touch of his hand on hers. She was suddenly anxious to see Roderick again, even though it meant braving the full force of Clive Hodge's condemnation.

"At least it's a pleasant day for another drive," she said. "Just wait a minute while I fetch my hat and some gloves."

He expressed admiration when she was as good as her word and returned almost as soon as she had left the room. "I didn't bring my curricle from Greystones this morning," he said. "But the pony and trap is already waiting for us downstairs."

He stood aside so that she could walk through the door of her suite, the sides of her crinoline brushing against the posts of the door. He hastened back to her side as soon as they were in the corridor.

"This staircase will be quicker, Elizabeth. My servant brought the pony-trap round to one of the side entrances and these stairs lead right to it."

She followed him without question. Danewood was so large that she still hadn't discovered more than half of its many entrances. There was one whole wing of the house, no longer used by the family, that Lord Danewood was just starting to restore. He claimed that he wished to display some of his art more advantageously. Elizabeth suspected that he merely wished to give employment to some of the labourers thrown out of work by the closing of the Danewood cloth manufactory.

The pony and trap were tethered to a post in a patch of warm sunshine. The earlier promise of a beautiful day had now been fulfilled and the sun shone from a sky of cloudless blue. A gentle wind, scarcely more than a breeze, ruffled the long grass and prevented the heat of the sun becoming oppressive.

She smiled at David as he handed her into the small carriage. "I'm glad we have to drive to the Vicarage, Cousin. I love the countryside around Danewood."

David whipped up the pony with unexpected force. "And yet Roderick is despoiling the land with unnecessary branch railway lines," he said. "The people have no work, the beauty of the land is destroyed, just so that he and a few fat investors in London may add some gold to their coffers."

She was surprised by the bitterness in his voice, although she had realised that David and his cousin didn't see eye to eye on the administration of Danewood.

"Oh no, David!" she said. "The railways cause hardship at first, but look at the benefits they bring in the end, especially to the poorer people who must work for a living. Our old cook told me that she was sent into service when she was twelve and after that she only saw her family when she went home for her mother's funeral. But now, with the railways, even our little scullery maid is able to return to her family for a visit. Five shillings for a return ticket to cover a distance of sixty miles—just think of it, David! She can pay for a visit to her family with only two months' wages."

"And in the meantime, the scullery-maid's father finds himself thrown out of work. Your logic is at fault, Elizabeth, which is only to be expected in a woman—especially one who is as pretty as you."

Elizabeth failed to appreciate the compliment. The blossoming hedgerows flashed by her unobserved. "Is that why you and Roderick don't get on?" she asked. "Because you disagree about the use of Danewood lands?"

David's grip on the pony's reins slipped for a moment, but he turned to her with an astonished smile. "Why, Cousin, you're imagining things, I'm sure. I have the greatest respect for Roderick and I certainly hope that respect is returned."

"Oh yes, yes, I'm sure it is. I didn't mean to imply..."

David laughed lightly. "Come on, Elizabeth. You see where this unsuitable conversation has led us? Let's return to more rewarding topics. When do you and Roderick leave for London?"

"As soon as possible," she said. "In fact, if the arrangements can be completed in time I believe Roderick plans to set off tomorrow. He plans to go by train." She bit her lip, sorry that she had re-introduced a controversial note.

"I see," David said, glossing over her reference to the train. "So soon? Then I really don't have any choice." He scowled angrily at some unspoken thought before turning to her with a reproachful gaze. "Clarissa Fanshawe loves me," he said and she could see tears of frustration beginning to form in his eyes. "It was easy to make her love me instead of *him*. I stopped that marriage. Why couldn't you be the same? I don't want to get rid of you."

"Get rid of me?" she repeated blankly. Had David somehow discovered that she and Lord Danewood weren't married? "It's difficult to get rid of a wife," she said tentatively, testing his knowledge.

"I know that," he said sadly. "I hoped to kill Roderick first, then we could have got married. But now...with the baby...it's no use. I'll have to get rid of you first and then Roderick. Today, before you leave for London."

The cold horror clutched at Elizabeth's stomach and she scarcely noticed that he began to caress her face with sad, trembling fingers. "Why...why must you get rid of us?"

He smiled at her sweetly, his fingers still tracing the outline of her cheeks. He explained patiently, as if to somebody who wasn't very clever. "I have to kill you now," he said, "or you'll both be off to London. When Roderick goes to London, I always stay and look after Danewood. So I will have no opportunity to kill either of you once you leave here."

She edged away from his caressing fingers, struggling to break free of his hold. "Don't be silly, David," she said still not quite able to accept the seriousness of his threats. Could any *real* conversation about death and destruction and murder be conducted in such a soft, even voice?

"I want you to drive me back to the Hall right away, or else I shall have to take over the reins."

"I'd take you back to the Hall if I could," he said. "But I went to all that trouble sending a message to the Hodges so that they'd stay in the Vicarage. And then I had to think of something to keep Roderick out of the way. *That* took some planning, I can tell you. I haven't much experience in setting fire to modern buildings." His face crumpled like a small child's. "I wanted you to enjoy your last drive with me, and you've spoiled it all with your questions. I didn't mean to tell you anything, so that you could die happy."

He jerked angrily on the reins and pulled the pony to a sharp halt. He sprang to the ground and tethered the reins to a sapling before Elizabeth could grab them.

"This is the spot I've chosen," he said as he slipped a bag of hay over the pony's nose. "The village lies just behind the crest of that rise. The woods protect us to the east and the hill and village to the north. But Roderick has granted a new right-of-way along the boundary line here, running from the village to the new railway station. It would be quite logical for some labourers to come upon you just at this point. Perhaps even

some navvies. A rape that went wrong, perhaps...."
He appeared lost in thought for a few seconds.

She felt the chill fingers of panic creep further up the bones of her spine. "I should like to drive on, David. Mr. and Mrs. Hodge are expecting us."

David frowned angrily at her words. "I've already told you that I invented that message from the Hodges. They aren't expecting us at all."

She no longer wondered if she had misunderstood his words. There was no doubt in her mind that she confronted a man teetering at the limits of his sanity. She tried to creep along the seat of the trap, into a position where she could seize the tethered reins. David saw her furtive movements and lunged for the carriage, dragging her out on to the ground. Quickly he pulled a small flask out of his pocket, uncorking it with one hand while with his other he held her pressed against the side of the pony-trap.

"Here!" he said, holding the bottle so that the sun was refracted from the liquid in a bright shower of light. "After you drink this you will be unconscious in a few minutes."

She pushed his hand roughly aside, dashing the glass to the ground. She was white and shaking with fury. "Are you mad?" she whispered. "Do you think *I'm* mad enough to help you kill me?"

He wouldn't release his hold on her, so he fumbled awkwardly as he bent down to pick up the broken glass. "It's all spilled," he said and his voice cracked on the edge of tears. He shook his head despairingly. "Now I don't have any more." He rounded on her in sudden rage, his hand lashing out to catch her a stinging blow on the head. "Why did you do that?" he screamed. "How am I going to stick a knife into you and beat your head in when you're awake?"

"Of course you won't be able to stick a knife into me," she said soothingly and tried not to let him see how the bile rose in her throat. "There's no need to kill me, David. I'm not really going to have a baby. That was just a story we made up, Roderick and I. You have to believe me. Danewood isn't going to have a new heir."

"Liar!" he yelled, before bringing his voice once more under control. "You're going to be the mother of Roderick's son," he said more quietly. "It's bound to be a son, you know. Everything always works out just right for Roderick, so it won't be a daughter."

"That's why you have to kill me, isn't it, David? Because the baby would inherit Danewood?"

"Yes," he agreed. "Danewood will be mine once you're all dead. I tried to save you, you can't say I didn't. I brought Clive Hodge here because I thought you might go back with him to Barclay Manor. I knew you'd run away from there to marry Roderick. I never believed that story about Liverpool. But I realise now that it's no use. You'll never marry me, even if I kill Roderick first. That's why I've decided to kill you. You made me do it. And tonight I shall poison Roderick. I'll make it look like suicide. People will believe it, you know, because they can all see he's crazy about you...Crazy..." He rolled the word round on his tongue, savouring its sound. "Yes," he said, satisfied. "Roderick is crazy about you, just as I'm crazy about Danewood."

In different circumstances she might have spared time to reflect on the irony of being killed by a madman because of a pregnancy that didn't exist. As it was she turned cautiously and tried once more to climb into the pony-trap, cursing her bulky skirts and petticoats which impeded every movement. David lunged for her, catching her easily and pushing her brutally on to the ground.

"You can't go into the carriage," he said. "I'm going to kill you over there, by the pathway."

"David, be reasonable. You can't kill me and then drive back to Danewood as though nothing had happened!"

He looked at her scornfully. "I shall say I saw thugs attacking you in the distance. I shall pretend you were already dead by the time I came upon you. I shall have to pretend they attacked me too, so that I won't be expected to identify anybody."

He put his hand to his head and winced in remembered pain. "I've only just recovered from the last wound I had to give myself, and that didn't convince Roderick somebody else was the enemy, so it was all in vain. Still, I won't have to hurt myself very much. I always turn faint at the sight of blood, so I shall look very pale when I ride back to the Hall." He looked at Elizabeth consideringly. "I expect you'll bleed quite a lot."

She didn't think there was any chance that his plan would work, particularly since Lord Danewood was already suspicious of his cousin. It was small consolation to know that David's crime would be punished. She had just discovered how badly she wanted to live. She had never even told Roderick how much she loved him and now that death seemed near she cursed the inhibitions which had kept them apart. If only she could release the pony there might be just a chance for her to escape.

It was a pathetic hope, of course. At the first movement of her knees, David jerked her to her feet. "I don't want to talk any more," he said. "I don't like talking to you now that I know you love Roderick. I liked it better in the beginning when I thought you'd married him for his money."

He reached into his pocket with one hand, although his other arm still held Elizabeth close to his side. His slight appearance, she realised with a fresh wave of despair, belied the wiry strength of his body. He spoke to Elizabeth pleadingly as he showed her the knife he had taken from his pocket.

"Don't make me hurt you, will you, Elizabeth? If you'll walk over to the woods, I'll find a branch and then I'll knock you out so that you won't feel anything. I promise." His voice cracked on a note of frantic turbulence. "Why did you spill that sleeping-draught? It would have made everything so *easy*."

She couldn't possibly cooperate in her own destruction. It was alien to every particle of her nature, so she lashed out at him with a ferocity that startled them both. The knife fell from his hand and they rolled on to the ground, David almost as impeded by the folds of her crinoline as she was herself. She fought with a power she had never known she possessed, but she was a woman and her strength was no match for David's. She knew it was only a matter of time before he finally subdued her. With the last of her strength, she struggled to ease out from under his body and to keep him out of reach of the knife.

She felt his hands close around her throat and she shut her eyes as she grappled feebly to remove them. Waves of red mist filled the screen behind her closed lids and she could feel consciousness slipping away from her. Her hands fell back limply to her sides, the red mist spread down from her head to the tips of her fingers and she knew that her power of resistance was gone.

She heard the crunching sound of bone meeting flesh in a shattering blow and she waited for the last shred of consciousness to leave her. The pain in her throat eased suddenly, but the red mist still floated in front of her eyes. She felt no pain from the blow she had heard so distinctly, and she wondered if she was already dead. She tried to open her eyes, curious to see where death had taken her.

A blinding light filled her vision, as though she were staring directly up towards the sun. In the centre of the aureole of light she could see the stern features of Clive Hodge wavering in and out of her vision. A tiny burst of laughter exploded in her brain. "Thank you, Lord," she whispered to herself, pleased, even in the midst of her despair, to find that the Almighty possessed a sense of humour. An angel disguised as Mr. Clive Hodge was certainly an amusing introduction to the terrors of Judgment.

The remaining wisps of red mist cleared in a flash of searing pain, and panic engulfed her. What if she had already been judged and this image of Clive Hodge had been sent not by the Lord but by the Devil? She tried to formulate a question, but all she could hear was the sound of somebody moaning. The vision of Mr. Clive Hodge began to speak.

"The wage of sin is death," he intoned. "And the reward of sin is eternal damnation."

The moaning noise stopped and she made a greater effort to focus her eyes. The moaning, she realised, had been coming from her. She rolled over, and by the exercise of considerable willpower, managed to raise herself up on one elbow. Mr. Hodge, she decided, was no vision, but very much a physical reality.

"Am I alive?" she croaked somewhat unnecessarily.

Clive Hodge peered at her distastefully, before turning away. "Physically, Lady Danewood, there is no doubt. But dead to all hope of salvation. Quite dead."

She had no energy for arguing her chances of eternal bliss. She was too happy to find that she was not in danger of being despatched to her reward—whatever that might be. "David?" she asked cautiously. Her throat was too sore for lengthy questions.

Clive Hodge pointed to a small huddle on the grass, guarded by the spry figure of his brother. Mr. Adolphus Hodge sprang to his feet and a faint flush of pride crept along his cheek bones.

"I knocked him out," he said, sounding almost as astonished as Elizabeth felt. "I used to have quite a good left-hook when I was a boy." He evidently decided that this wasn't an accomplishment for a minister to boast of, so he added earnestly, "I trust you are not seriously hurt, Lady Danewood?"

"Not too much," she said faintly.

Clive Hodge had already regained his normal sepulchral manner and he said mournfully, "The Lord moves in mysterious ways, his wonders to perform."

"Yes," said Elizabeth fervently, finding herself for once in absolute agreement with Mr. Hodge. "Please would you drive me home now, before Mr. Vincent comes round?"

Clive Hodge looked at the prostrate form of David Vincent, then back up at Elizabeth. "Mr. Vincent is certainly a sinner, but then on the other hand so are you. The Bible encourages us to shun the company of sinners, you know. Besides, you have lost your bonnet and your dress is torn. Whatever would people say if I escorted you back to the Hall looking like this?"

"I'm quite sure everybody would simply say thank you," said Mr. Adolphus Hodge with the merest trace of irritation. "Here, Lady Danewood, allow me to place this travelling rug around your shoulders."

He pulled a tartan plaid from inside the pony-trap and Elizabeth huddled herself willingly within its folds. Her whole body was shaking now despite the warmth of the day and she was happy to clutch the rug around her. Adolphus Hodge unhitched the pony and checked the couplings to the trap, while she clambered into the carriage on limbs almost too shaky to support her.

Mr. Hodge handed the reins to his brother. "You had better drive Lady Danewood to the Hall, Clive, because I have to stay and guard...watch over...Mr. Vincent. And please send somebody from the Hall to assist me as soon as possible."

He waited for Clive to climb up into the driver's

seat, then administered a sharp slap to the pony's rump. The pony, still chewing on the remnants of a flake of hay, seemed totally indifferent to the scenes of high drama recently enacted at its feet, and moved reluctantly.

Adolphus Hodge came up to the carriage just before the pony finally started its trot back towards the Hall.

"We must thank God for your safety, Lady Danewood. Today is the first time that I have ever chosen to take this path on my Sunday afternoon walk."

"Thank God indeed," said Elizabeth hoarsely.

"Lady Danewood..." He spoke her name as if the words were torn from him. "Was Mr. Vincent really trying to *kill* you?"

"Yes," said Elizabeth and astonished herself by bursting into tears. "He was really trying to kill me."

THIRTEEN

Mr. Hodge was probably as relieved as Elizabeth when the pink marble steps of Danewood Hall came into view. He had exhausted his store of biblical quotations suitable for admonishing hysterical females (after all, how many were there?). Elizabeth, for her part, had given up her efforts to stop weeping. She decided, to the accompaniment of Mr. Hodge's announcement that the Devil walketh about as a hungry lion, seeking whom he may devour, that attempted murder was sufficient cause for a display of feminine sensibility.

The butler's horrified exclamations as she tumbled from the pony-trap on to the steps of the portico would have given some indication of her battered appearance had either she or Mr. Hodge been in a fit state to listen. But she was too weary to absorb what the butler was saying and dismissed his questions with a vague gesture of her arm. "Lord Danewood!" she croaked, through a throat inflamed almost beyond the point where speech was possible. "Ask him to come." She sank down in a huddle on the marble steps.

"He's gone to the railway station, m'lady." Barnet's distress was evident as he deferentially scooped his mistress back on to her feet and sent a scurrying footman to find Mrs. Smithers or Janet. He led her into the hallway and said, "Please sit here, my lady, until your maid arrives. Whatever has happened, my lady?"

She ignored the butler's remarks. She only had energy for following a single train of thought. "Lord Danewood has gone to the *railway station?*" Elizabeth was aware of feeling an irrational resentment. David Vincent had tried to murder her, and *he* had taken himself off to the railway station! She tried to tell herself that her irritation had nothing to do with the fact that she was longing to throw herself into his arms and sob out her story against the comforting warmth of his strong shoulders.

"The station's been set on fire, m'lady." The butler looked at her doubtfully, wondering how much gory detail she was capable of absorbing in her present state. "His lordship had to go, m'lady. You know there's been some trouble in the village over the new railway and the villagers would just have left the buildings to burn. Lord Danewood had to organize the village folk to fight the fire, or he wouldn't be able to bring in supplies for his new factory. And the village folk need that factory, even if they don't realise it yet."

"I suppose David caused the fire as well," she said dully, too conscious of her bruised body and aching throat to care about exercising discretion. "He set the fire to get Roderick out of the way. No wonder he said it needed some planning!"

She looked up and saw both Janet and Mrs. Smithers hurrying down the long corridor. She had never thought their bustling figures could be so welcome. She managed to struggle to her feet and turned to Clive Hodge, who had been waiting in uncharacteristic silence beside her chair. "Thank you, Mr. Hodge," she said, offering him her hand. "You and your brother saved my life, you know."

"Blessed are the peacemakers," he intoned pontifically, preparing to launch into a short sermon. Some uncomfortable thought occurred to him, however, and he fell abruptly silent. Perhaps he realised, thought Elizabeth, that the use of a strong left-hook to David Vincent's chin could hardly be considered the action of a peacemaker.

She managed to remain on her feet until the two maids arrived at her side. At the touch of Mrs. Smithers' muscular arm around her waist, she gave up the battle to remain conscious. A final thought struck her just as the folds of welcome blackness rippled over her.

"David!" she croaked. "He's still out on the hill!"

A distant roaring noise pierced the darkness of her oblivion, approaching swiftly and tearing through the protective veil of her dreams. The devil, she thought, remembering Clive Hodge's words. He is seeking whom he may devour. She opened her eyes quickly and discovered to her relief that she was in her own bed. She could see Janet and Mrs. Smithers hovering nervously at the entrance to her bedroom.

The roaring noise had not diminished in volume even though she had opened her eyes. It came, she realised, from Lord Danewood. He was storming down the corridor demanding at the top of his lungs why, in a house full of servants, his wife had been left unattended and open to murderous attacks. A trailing entourage of servants was failing to provide him with satisfactory answers to his questions. Janet and Mrs. Smithers were shaking visibly.

Elizabeth struggled to pull herself up into a sitting position. She was discovering new bruises with every movement she tried to make. "Roderick!" she called out huskily. Her throat was excruciatingly painful, burning inside and deeply bruised on the outside, but she wanted to distract his attention from the hapless servants.

At the sound of her voice he strode over to her side, crushing her to him with a total indifference to the presence of several maids and numerous footmen. "Oh my darling!" he murmured. "How could I ever have been fool enough to expose you to such danger?"

She was glad that the presence of an audience forced her to keep her head. The temptation to collapse into his arms in a sobbing heap was very strong. "That was the whole purpose of your plan, Roderick," she said too quietly for the servants to hear.

"Don't remind me of my folly!" His heart was beating so fast that he might have been running, and the hands which stroked her hair were far from steady. She tried to ignore the delicious sensation of lassitude that was creeping insidiously over her. "The servants!" she protested, not because she really cared but as a warning to herself not to lose her head.

He was looking deep into her eyes and didn't bother to turn his head. "They have certainly had the tact to remove themselves by now," he said. She managed to tear her gaze away and saw with a flash of panic that the crowd around her doorway had melted entirely away. She and Lord Danewood were alone.

He untied the ribbons of her robe, and pulled apart the folds of her nightgown so that he could examine her injuries more closely. She winced when his fingers traced the chain of bruises around her neck. They were already darkening to purple and the imprint of David's fingers was clearly visible at each side of her throat. She concentrated on the pain of her bruises, so that she could forget the pleasure of his touch.

Roderick's arms tightened convulsively around her. "Oh God! When I returned just now and learned what had happened to you, I thought I would go mad with self-reproach." His voice trembled with emotion. "Can you possibly forgive me?"

She allowed herself to relax against the strength of his shoulders for a brief moment, then gently eased herself out of his embrace.

"You smell of smoke," she said.

He was not put off by her change of subject. "I've been fighting a fire," he said impatiently. "Adolphus Hodge came running down to the station to tell me what had happened to you and I came straight back to Danewood." He put his fingers under her chin, turning her face up so that she couldn't hide from his searching gaze. "No forgiveness, Elizabeth?"

"There's nothing to forgive," she said, trying to sound matter-of-fact. "You can't be held responsible for the actions of a madman."

"No. But I should have told you of my suspicions," he said. "I couldn't bring myself to accuse my own cousin without proof. It's not easy to believe that a childhood companion is planning to murder you."

She looked away from the glimpse of anguish she saw in his eyes. "Where is David?" She asked the question painfully. "Will you have to inform the magistrate?"

"David is dead," he answered. His voice was flat but she knew him well enough to recognize the unspoken torment behind the brusque words. "Clive Hodge sent out the servants to help Adolphus bring him back to Danewood, but he was already dead."

"H-how did he die?" She swallowed over the painful swelling in her throat. "You did say, didn't you, that Adolphus Hodge was unharmed?"

"The Vicar has suffered nothing more than bruised knuckles, thank God. However, he feels very guilty because David managed to slash his wrists with his pocketknife before Adolphus even realised that he'd regained consciousness."

Lord Danewood cradled Elizabeth in his arms as she burst into tears. "Hush, my love! If David had lived he would have been hanged or confined as a lunatic. Remember that he tried to use that knife on you—and for no other reason than the fact that you stood between him and his crazed ambition to possess Danewood."

She started to laugh, on the verge of hysteria. "And all for nothing!" Sobs and hiccuping bursts

217

of laughter alternately shook her slender body. "If only he had known there was no Danewood heir, not even a Lady Danewood!"

He seized her firmly by the shoulders. "There soon will be a Lady Danewood," he said. "And as for the Danewood heir, that too can be taken care of."

Her hysterical outburst ceased abruptly. "I realise that you feel sorry for me, Lord Danewood. But you have no need to exaggerate your responsibility for my situation. It's time for this masquerade to end."

"I agree. It's high time for this absurd situation to be brought to a close."

She felt sure that her cheeks turned pale, but she did her best to speak calmly. "We shall have to change our original plans, my lord. Clive Hodge will certainly tell my parents that I'm living here. I won't just be able to disappear abroad."

He drew away from her in bewilderment. "What *are* you talking about? I thought I had already fought this battle and won it. A special licence is waiting for us in London. As far as I'm concerned, our marriage is due to take place on Wednesday." His face was grim as he added, "There is one good result of David's attack upon you. We can claim that his brutal actions brought on a miscarriage. The mythical heir is thus disposed of and we can produce a real one at our leisure."

"But it's not only the baby... You don't have to make noble gestures because you feel sorry for me."

"I am *not* marrying you because I'm sorry for you." His grey eyes were suddenly flooded with the warmth of hidden laughter. "I'm marrying you because Sam has threatened to leave me if I don't. You can't condemn me to a life without Sam."

She wished she could answer him with a smile. "I understand that losing Sam would be a terrible blow. But a lifetime tied to the wrong woman is scarcely a recipe for happiness."

His eyes were as unreadable as if he had worn his darkened spectacles. "What makes you so certain you're the wrong woman? You know how well you've fitted into life at Danewood, so it must be because of your feelings for me."

She looked up quickly at the note of hesitancy in his voice. Was it possible that he didn't realise the state of her emotions? Didn't he know that her bones turned to water every time he touched her, and that her heart stopped beating every time he looked at her with the full force of his piercing gaze?

She was breathless with shyness when she answered him. "I don't think my feelings will change, Roderick. Deepen, perhaps, but not change."

"Elizabeth?" This time there was no mistaking the painful uncertainty as he whispered her name. "Are you telling me that despite everything I've done, you still love me just a little?"

"No," she said, then relented when she saw the pain sweep across his face. "I'm not trying to tell you I love you a little. I love you very much, more than I ever imagined I could love any man."

He didn't answer her with words, but swept her into his arms and showered kisses over her face and shoulders. Strangely enough, she was aware of no pain from her bruises.

As if revived by her embrace, he sprang off the bed, his normal arrogance of manner entirely restored. "You must hurry up and get better," he said. "We need to leave for London tomorrow if we are to be married on Wednesday."

"Yes, my lord," she said meekly.

"On Thursday we shall go to Barclay and pay a visit to your parents before leaving on our delayed honeymoon." He saw her start of surprise, and his face softened into a smile. "I know how much you want to see your mother and, since we can hardly invite her to the wedding, I thought this would be the next best thing. Besides, I can't help thinking you will stand up to Papa better if you have the security of knowing we're legally married."

"Thank you, my lord." This time there was no mockery in her reply. She was touched by his thoughtfulness, although when she was with Lord Danewood, even Papa faded into insignificance.

"And finally, until I have you safely tied to me by the bonds of matrimony, you are to send me hourly messages reassuring me that you still love me."

"*Hourly* messages, my lord?"

"Hourly," he said inexorably. "At least during daylight hours."

She didn't answer, but closed her eyes and uttered a low moan of pain. "Roderick...Please ...come...here..."

He rushed to her side. "Elizabeth, my darling! What is it?"

She opened her eyes and stretched out her hand to touch his cheek. "I am only obeying your orders, my lord." She slipped her arms around his neck and looked at him, her eyes shining with happiness.

"Roderick," she said softly. "I love you."